Red Sword

Bora Chung

Translated by Anton Hur

PAN

First published 2019 in Korean as 붉은 칼
This English translation first published 2025 by Honford Star
This edition published 2026 by Pan
an imprint of Pan Macmillan Publishing India Private Limited
707 Kailash Building
26 K. G. Marg, New Delhi 110001
www.panmacmillan.co.in

Pan Macmillan, The Smithson, 6 Briset Street, Farringdon, London EC1M 5NR
Associated companies throughout the world
www.panmacmillan.com

ISBN 978-93-6113-777-8

2

Printed and bound in India by Manipal Technologies, Manipal

FSC
www.fsc.org
MIX
Paper | Supporting responsible forestry
FSC® C043100

Contents

1. *Ghosts in the Fog*

The young man was beautiful. It was underlit and stuffy inside the spaceship, and no one knew what the future would bring, and she, the young woman, was afraid. She spent many days crouched in the dark with the young man. The Imperials did not say much about the enemy, only referring to them as "white monsters" that had invaded the Empire's territory. What these monsters really were, she knew not. The only certainty was that no answer would be forthcoming should she ask.

What the monsters were wasn't important. The Imperials said that if they helped vanquish the monsters, the colonized would be given their freedom. She couldn't believe everything the Imperials said. But freedom—that was a seductive word. A word that upon hearing exuded a whiff of hope. A wisp of a thing that persisted in the air around them once it was uttered, a strand of weak light they fixed their gaze on. A hope.

This was why, along with the other women, she had boarded the spaceship. She called these women "unnis," for they were like older sisters to her. The unnis told her the Imperials could not be trusted. For all they knew, the colonized in this ship were being sold off to another planet, or even farther out across some unimaginable distance, to another galaxy. It wasn't as if she didn't suspect this herself; the thought had crossed her mind as well. But they had mentioned *freedom*. She had to at least try. And if she failed at the attempt, there was always her sword. The Imperials had not confiscated it, perhaps because they didn't know what it was. The sleek velvet scabbard and the elaborately embroidered patterns on its surface, with the little mirrors sewn into it and the dangling flower and butterfly charms, had likely made them think it was some kind of decorative bauble toted by women. They couldn't imagine the long and fiercely beautiful blade sheathed within. She had boarded the vessel gripping her red velvet scabbard, the sword hidden inside.

And then the young man had come to her.

Unlike the Imperials, who were rough and menacing beasts, the young man was quiet and gentle. His skin, which had darkened in the sun, returned to its light brown as they spent their long days in the dim bowels of the vessel. He had red hair on both his head and body. She had only known black hair and brown eyes, which made the young man's red hair and dark hazel eyes surprising, as well as the red hair on his body when he revealed his nakedness, and the young man became shy at her surprise. When she wrapped his genitals with her hands, the young man closed his eyes and opened his lips. His penis was soft, and in her mouth it tasted slightly sour and bitter and soon hardened. The young man, as if enduring pain, screwed his eyes shut, grit his teeth, and gripped her shoulders. When she held out her hand, he grabbed it with his long and rough fingers and threw his head back. Long after those moments had passed, from time to time she would remember the sound of the young man's quick breathing, and a heat would rise up from within her.

The young man's language was inscrutable to her and he likewise knew hardly any of hers, which was why they eventually came up with a language that met in the middle. His situation wasn't very different from hers. The Imperials had charged into his village and taken it over. When the young man was born, his planet was already in the hands of the Empire. His father was forced to work the mines, where he was eventually beaten to death by the Imperials, and when the young man's mother was caught teaching him how to fire a gun, the Imperials had dragged her away to be executed. After witnessing her death, the young man was thrown onto the spaceship for the reason that he knew how to use a gun.

"Never be able to go back home," the young man said. "No one and nothing for me there, anyway."

Still, there was a glint deep in the young man's eye, as if he had hidden a blade there.

Which was why she showed him the blade hidden in her velvet scabbard.

Like the Imperials, the young man knew of guns, but he didn't know what a sword was. As the long and thin blade gleamed against the dim light reflected against the inner hull of the spaceship, the young man, seduced, held out his hand as if to touch it. Afraid he would injure himself, she grabbed his hand.

That had been the first time. His hand was hard and rough. And warm.

His lips were warm and soft.

Against that cold and dark hull, the young man was led to lay down next to the sword wrapped in velvet. He knew all of her wounds and scars and the imperfections of her skin, which was why when she opened her body to him he checked, several times, if he could, if she was really all right with it, and if she truly wanted it. Whenever he did, she smiled and said yes, it was fine, she wanted it. And she embraced him. The young man was passionate and desperate, and he grit his teeth as if the act of taking her was not one of pleasure but of pain. Which was why it was her turn to ask him if he were all right, and he answered that he loved her.

And as soon as the young man disembarked from the spaceship, he was killed.

The world the spaceship had landed on was white. The patch of sky above was an off-white gray, and white fog obscured everything else in sight. It even rolled over the ground, making it impossible to tell what the terrain looked like. Clearly there was an atmosphere, but could humans breathe this air? She took a few experimental deep breaths. Immediately, she started coughing. The fog tasted of iron, and every breath made her throat and chest constrict painfully.

It wasn't just her. Everyone around her breathing the air as it came through the hatch was coughing. She heard murmurs of, *Ugh, what is this, I'm going to suffocate.*

"Get out!" shouted the Imperials. One of them came up to her and roughly pushed her back. She stumbled out of the hatch, almost losing her grip on her sword. The young man quickly came to her side and took her hand. She managed to regain her balance, and the two of them walked out into the white world outside the ship.

Their feet disappeared into fog. They couldn't see more than an inch in front of them.

"I can't see anything," mumbled the young man as he looked around. He sounded worried. "I can't use my gun like this . . ."

Those were his last words. In the very next moment, a white ray of light cut through the fog and diagonally sliced through the young man, from his shoulder to his hip. The right side of his body slid off his left and fell into the fog without a sound. The left side silently followed suit.

She screamed but even that sound was almost muffled in the fog. She dropped to her knees by the body of the young man, just before another white ray of light flashed by where her head had been. She ducked into the white fog.

The young man's left eye was next to her. No blood flowed from the sliced body. The cross-section where the light had passed through him had been cauterized. His face was pale, his lips slightly open. She remembered the first time their lips had touched, the first time their hands touched, and the first time she accepted him inside her and how he had closed his eyes and thrown his head back and opened his mouth like it was open now. She remembered but felt nothing. Her mind and her heart were filled with the white fog. She shed no tears, and no more screams came forth. She slowly raised her numb body.

There was a white ghost in front of her. She realized that the form wearing white clothes, surrounded by white fog, was one of the "monsters" they had told her about.

But the monster did not seem anything like a monster. It was noticeably taller than most human men she knew. There were two arms, and while mostly obscured by the fog, two legs, and a head on a pair of shoulders, giving it the overall look of a human. But its head was completely wrapped inside something white and translucent, and through that she could not even see a trace of a face. She stared up at where its facial features ought to be.

On top of the white thing around its head was a third "arm." The arm held a white wand, its intensely white and shining tip aimed at her face. Without a moment to think, she held up her scabbard.

From the tip of the monster's white wand came a blinding white ray of light, which bounced off the scabbard and hit the monster's legs. A thick, gray smoke wafted up. The monster looked down at where the smoke came from. And just like the young man had done before, it silently fell into the white fog.

She didn't hesitate. She struck down at the third arm protruding from the fallen monster's head. The third arm dropped the white wand it was holding. She snatched it up and leaped backward at almost the same time.

The monster, with its other two arms, tried to get up on its uninjured leg. She pointed the white wand at the monster. The monster froze.

Nothing happened. She didn't know how to activate it. No matter how much she pressed on the bump on the handle or whipped it in the air, the white wand didn't respond.

The monster's translucent helmet made it difficult to see the white face of the monster inside, but she sensed there was something of a smile of relief there.

She stuck the useless white wand to her belt and drew her sword from its sheath.

Red Sword

The white monster rose. Its left arm went to its back, where it drew out another white wand.

This time, the wand didn't shoot rays of light. Instead, a white blaze burst upward like the blade of a sword.

Carefully, she covered her face with the scabbard. That white blade was sure to slice her in half like the ray had done to the young man. Would the light also slice through the sword or damage it? She had to keep such possibilities in mind. She only had the one sword after all.

But there was one thing that was as clear as day: that white light ray was a weapon. And when it had hit the mirrors on the scabbard, it had bounced off. The fact that the mirror happened to be angled toward the monster's legs was just coincidence. Sheer luck.

She held up the scabbard with her left hand, stretched out her sword with her right, and charged at the monster's legs.

On the monster's left leg was a dark gray crack, and from the crack flowed a white liquid. Was the monsters' blood also white? The sight of the white blood made her head swim, and she wanted to throw up.

A quick shake of her head restored her self-control, and she protected her face with her scabbard as she attacked the monster's legs with her sword. The tip of her sword lodged itself in the monster's white thigh.

The monster let out a strained scream as it swung its ray of white light down toward her head. She unstuck her sword and quickly retreated backwards. The tip of her sword had broken off. It was lodged in the leg of the monster, and this time there was no white blood coming out of it.

The monster trained its ray at her again. Her sword tip lodged in its leg didn't seem to affect it at all. Perhaps its covering was armor.

If so, her only weapon, the sword, would be useless against it. And with the tip gone, she couldn't pierce it, either.

She felt a searing burn and let out a scream. The white ray of light had grazed her left wrist. She had almost dropped the scabbard, but she managed to hold onto it and turn the side with the mirrors toward the monster. The pillar of light bounced off the mirror and flew over the monster's head.

Without giving her a chance to even glance at her injured wrist, the monster pointed the white pillar of light at her as it charged. She stumbled backward. Everything on the ground was covered in a layer of white fog; she had no way of knowing what she had stumbled over.

Amid her confusion, the monster caught up to her and held the white pillar up over her head. The moment it struck down to slice her in half, she leaped toward the monster and sliced it in the belly sideways, jumping away to her left.

The blade of the tipless sword had sliced the monster like paper. White liquid gushed out of the wound.

Still holding the wand that emitted the white pillar of light, the monster stared down at its own stomach.

And in the next moment, it collapsed into the white fog.

She approached the monster. She prodded it with her foot.

The monster slowly turned its head. She could see, through its spherical helmet, the vague outlines of its face.

She crouched. Wrapping her hands on the helmet, she pulled it off. She wanted to see the monster's face. To see what she was fighting and what kind of thing would kill the young man.

The monster was a woman. If this species even had such distinctions. The lines of its subtle and smooth features felt feminine to her.

She was breathing shallowly. Her chest was rapidly going up and down, and the lips of her white mouth were wide open. Her skin was so white it had a slight tint of blue, and her hair and eyebrows were all white. Her pupils also looked white at first glance, but they were actually the very light blue-gray of the sky of this planet.

These light blue-gray eyes were looking at her. She looked back.

White liquid spurted from her mouth.

She kept staring.

Soon, nothing came out of that white mouth. The blue-gray pupils of the white woman's eyes remained fixed on her and no longer moved.

From its hand, she removed the white wand.

The Imperials seemed to set their weapons to biometric information, which made their weapons useless to their enemies if they happened to be stolen. She suspected the white wands worked under the same principle. She tried to take the long gloves off the white woman, but they seemed to be connected to the armor, and there was no seam she could find. She tried putting the wand into the dead woman's hand.

The wand turned white. When she pressed it, the white ray shone out.

She couldn't help smiling. For in that moment, she was

remembering a story the young man had told her about his childhood.

"My mother and I made bullets together. We melted lead and poured it into molds ..."

The ground began to shake, and the memory of his story vanished as swiftly as it had appeared. She looked around.

To the right of the body there were five white aliens standing in two lines.

She didn't move. With her hand still gripping the wand in the dead woman's grip, she stared at the two lines of whites.

The white standing at the very front pressed a device on their leg, which made the ground vibrate. They seemed to be the leader of the group; whenever they put their hand on the device, it sent vibrations into the ground, which would stop when they took their hand off it. It seemed to be a signal of some kind, but she didn't understand it.

She stayed still. The white leader pressed the device and made the ground vibrate again. The four standing behind the leader immediately surrounded the body in neat formation. They moved quickly and precisely.

They had to have been trained people. They were nothing like the barbaric and backward indigenous monsters that the Imperials insisted they were.

When one of them seemed to realize she was gripping the white wand using the white woman's hand, they aimed at her. Still crouched, she held up both her hands hoping that the international Earth gesture for surrender would be understood on this planet as well.

Her sword and scabbard were behind her.

Her hands still in the air, she sat back on the ground. Keeping herself low but slightly lifting her behind from the ground, she slowly moved away from the body of the dead white woman.

She felt the scabbard bump on her behind. Her sword was a little further back. A little more backward, just a little more to the left . . .

One of the white figures shot a ray of light. It just missed her, and she grabbed her sword and scabbard and began to run. A white ray grazed her shoulder, leaving a burn. As she screamed, another ray brushed past her leg. She fell.

Three of the white aliens guarded the dead white woman as the other two approached her. Not taking her eyes off them, she gripped her scabbard—that was when she realized her hand was injured. She held the scabbard in her injured right hand and grabbed the hilt of the sword in her left hand, squeezing as hard as she could. One of the white figures aimed their white wand at her. She never looked away.

A bang. The white alien aiming at her veered as if hit on the shoulder. Another shot. They fell.

The white alien left standing looked down at their companion, confused. She quickly got to her feet. Before the remaining white alien could hold up their weapon, she had her sword ready.

"Drop your light weapon!" a man shouted from behind her. "Drop it now, or I will shoot again!"

Her sword still at the ready, she glanced behind her. It was one of the older men who had been in the spaceship with her, aiming a gun at the white aliens. Behind him through the fog, she could just about discern some colorful scabbards.

The unnis. The unnis were here.

Her sword still up and ready, she started to back toward them.

Just then, the white alien that had been shot got up on their feet.

A monstrous sight. The white alien who had fallen into the obscuring fog had got up and was slowly walking toward them. In a leisurely manner, they extracted the bullet from their chest, then from their stomach. They looked at the bullets as if fascinated and opened a container on their wrist to drop them in. When the bullets were dropped, the container automatically closed.

Then, the white aliens lifted their white wands and aimed at her and her people.

She raised her sword aloft.

"Your swords!" she shouted. "Guns are useless, use your swords!"

As the men stood confused, the women stepped forward.

The white rays bounced off their scabbards and back to where the dead woman lay. This made two of the three white aliens that guarded the body run to them. The four white aliens and the five women with swords each stood their ground, keeping each other's weapons in sight. She raised her scabbard high.

The ground vibrated, startling the sword-bearing women. She kept her scabbard in the air and signaled for the others to wait and see.

The white alien guarding the dead woman came forth. Like she had done before, they held up their two hands, showing they were not armed. And then, they pressed the device on their leg again. The ground gently vibrated once more.

The white aliens slowly lowered their weapons.

The women also, slowly, lowered their swords.

Not taking their eyes off the women and their swords, the white aliens picked up their fallen compatriot and disappeared into the fog.

Even after they were gone, it took a moment for the silence to be broken.

"What happened?" said one of the women. The older man asked what had become of the young man.

"Are you hurt?" another woman inquired.

She did not cry. But she couldn't answer either. She opened her mouth to speak but ended up shuddering instead.

The other women supported her. They sheathed her sword in her scabbard, avoided her wounds as they placed her hands on their shoulders and surrounded her, and walked her back to where the spaceship was.

The Imperials clucked their tongues at the fact that they hadn't brought back any of the white aliens' weapons. But the women didn't bother telling them of everything that had happened to them, and the Imperials only said of their apparent lack of thinking, "Typical women," and let them go as they shook their heads.

Even after her wounds were treated, the woman kept shivering. The women suggested she eat, but all she could manage to take in was a little water. She couldn't bear even the thought of food. She couldn't forget the young man's left eye as it stared back at her through the fog. The dark hazel had already turned black and there was no life in it, and the slightly open, pale lips were as beautiful as they had been when he was alive. The young man had grown up in suffering and had spent six years, a lifetime for a youth, getting to this faraway planet in search of his freedom, but he had accomplished none of what he'd set out to do and died a senseless death. Why did he have to be born, and why did he have to die?

Amid these thoughts, she realized that she had nothing that had belonged to the boy. Which was why she left the spaceship once more in search of his body.

The planet's sky was a constant whitish gray, making it difficult to tell night from day. As they traversed the black of space, the crew of the vessel she had come in with had observed strict rules where leaving one's bunk, let alone quarters, during sleeping hours was forbidden. But perhaps because they had arrived at their destination and the battle had already begun, no one stopped her from leaving the ship.

Her arms, right shoulder, and right leg, all places where the white rays had touched, were burning and aching. The smell of metal in the white fog was even more stinging than before. She had no idea where the body of the young man was. Soon, she was lost.

—It's all right.

It was the young man's voice.

—I'm here.

She walked toward it. A hand was stretched out, which she grabbed. Rough and warm, just as she remembered it.

"Aren't you hurt?" she asked. The young man grinned.

—It hurts very much.

She started to cry. The tears she hadn't shed when the young man had fallen, when she had killed the white woman, or when the unnis came running to her aid—they poured from her all at once. She gripped the warm and rough hand of the young man and kept crying and crying.

—It's all right.

The young man kept saying.

—It's all right.

His words made her cry even more.

The young man waited patiently until she stopped crying. Once she did, he started to speak again.

—Take my gun.

She tried to control her voice. "I don't know how to use—"

—Take it anyway.

He smiled.

—Who else will ever remember me in this world?

This made her start crying again.

—You'll survive.

He patted the back of her hand.

—You'll survive until the end and find what you've always searched for.

"But how ..." She was whispering through her sobs. "How will I, alone, without you ..."

—You can do it. Because you're strong.

Smiling, he carefully wiped the tears running down her cheeks.

—And you're with strong people.

"But I'm not strong," she cried, "I'm not strong without you ..."

And she told him all the stories she had told him before about her wounds and traces on her skin. How she had been born and raised to use and guard the sword, the battle when the Imperials had conquered her village, the violent memories of everyone she had loved being killed or dragged away somewhere, and the other violence endured at the hands of the Imperials, the life of a prisoner of war, the life of a slave. Every time she experienced these violent things, a little bit of her mind and soul would crumble, and she did not feel she was getting stronger. She simply felt more exhausted. The only time in her whole life when she had felt truly strong was the time she had spent with the young man. It was her happiest time.

—It's all right.

The young man consoled her again.

—You'll be happy again, and strong again.

He let go of her hand and stood up.

"What do you mean? Where are you going?"

Fear gripped her. The young man, gently, smiled.

—I have to go. Because I'm dead. You're still alive; I can't be with you all the time anymore.

"No. Don't go," she begged. "Don't go—"

—It's all right.

He handed her the gun again.

—And don't forget my gun.

She took it from him. The gun felt like the young man had in her hand, hard but warm.

The young man smiled and kissed her forehead.

—Kill the Imperials with it.

Startled, she woke. Tears dampened her pillow. And underneath the pillow was the young man's gun.

She took it out and stroked it. The surface was rough, the steel was hard, and it was warm like the young man's hand.

She put it back under her pillow.

Kill the Imperials with it.

She began to think.

Double Helix I

Where does consciousness come from? Does human identity arise from memory? Does transplanting memories into a cultured meat make it human?

These were the original questions.

Snails sensitized to electric shocks showed responses of retracting themselves for fifty seconds when researchers tapped the ground next to them. In contrast, snails that hadn't received electric conditioning showed only a second of retraction. RNA was extracted from the shocked snails and injected into the unconditioned ones, and when these supposedly unconditioned snails felt the researchers tapping their environs, they retracted themselves for a long time despite never having been shocked.

That was the first experiment.

Could human memories be transplanted?

Many experiments had to be conducted to find the answer to this question.

Some animals died during the experiments while others lost their minds. And some animals didn't respond to the experiments at all. The researchers decided to create animals that were convenient to experiment on. Subjects that could remember and respond like humans, the creation of which might eventually lead to the first completely artificial human being. If we could transplant human memories into a clone, human beings could live forever without losing their spiritual or biological humanity.

The black birds created in the lab attacked them. They didn't seem to be receptive of the memories of other animals. Not in the way the researchers wanted them to be, at any rate. But it took a long time for them to realize this failure.

The black birds remembered the researchers. They seemed to remember them from the moment the first black bird opened its eyes. It wasn't born of an egg. The researchers cracked the plastic shell for it, taking it out. After the feathers had dried out and the bird could spread its wings, it looked upon the researchers in a wary manner. But the black bird then was still small, and they hadn't had a long time to observe it yet. They didn't know enough about it to determine whether its wariness was from being a newborn life with no mother in sight or the natural anxiety of all small animals.

The black bird could soon move and walk—flying took a little more time and effort. The researchers chalked it up as a success. They made more artificial eggs to produce more black birds. And as the black birds incubated in their plastic shells, they implanted a tracking device in the first black bird and let it fly out into the white sky.

2. *Dirty River*

They set out at dawn. The prisoners walked, and the Imperials herded them as they flew about in their small flying machines.

They walked through the endless white fog. No one knew where they were headed. Never mind their destination, they could barely see what was right in front of them. The patch of sky ahead was dim and pale, with an occasional cold blue that broke through the cloud cover and shifted into light violet, finally succumbing back to the weak gray cloudiness of when they first arrived. The fog was increasingly dense and moist. A damp chill seeped through their skin down to their bones.

A woman in a deep indigo skirt was walking by her. She didn't know her well but knew her to be the mate of the woman in the light green skirt. The Imperials were weary of any of the prisoners befriending each other. But the prisoners understood one another because they were prisoners, and there was nothing anyone could do from preventing two people from feeling close to one another. Having woken up from a deep sleep and thrust into a strange world where death was surely lying in wait, they needed someone to lean on. Everyone had understood that the young man had been her mate, just as everyone knew the woman in the deep indigo skirt and the woman in the light green skirt were a pair.

"Where is your mate?" she asked in a low voice.

"Behind us."

The two continued to walk. The other prisoners were also presumably walking, but they could only see whoever was right next to them.

In the terrain before them there would perhaps be death. Shrouded by the white fog, each of them were alone.

She longed for the young man. She thought of his gun holstered against her thigh underneath her skirt.

The ground vibrated. Once, then twice.

The vibrations spread down the line of prisoners making their way through the dust and fog.

"Halt!" They could just about make out the voice of the older man, speaking in the language of the Empire. "I said, halt! River ahead!"

They could tell he was shouting with all his might, but he sounded very far away. She immediately understood the word "river" and stopped in her tracks.

She couldn't see anything in front of her. Crouching down, she felt around with her hands. Dirt and thin blades of grass with a sticky texture wrapped around her fingers. Still crouched, she continued to advance forward, feeling the ground as she went.

Liquid. Heavier and stickier than the river water she knew on Earth, but liquid. She rubbed the liquid between her hands, carefully feeling it with her palms, as she stood up.

A dull explosion from behind. Flashes of light, splattering of dirt. Startled, she almost fell into the river.

—Attack!

The order came from one of the flying Imperials above, just as the Imperials started shooting at the prisoners from their machines.

—Attack! Anyone who does not shall be deemed a traitor and executed!

"But we're blocked by water!" shouted the older man in Imperial. "We do not know what lurks in its depths or how deep it is, how are we to throw ourselves into it?"

In lieu of an answer, the Imperials fired. Some of the charges hit the water with a splash, lighting up the surrounding fog.

—Attack!

The order was a bark issued from the floating vehicles above.

Hesitantly, the prisoners began walking into the river. She gritted her teeth and stepped in as well. The water was neither cold nor warm. It was heavier than the water on Earth and wrapped itself around her ankles, making it difficult to walk through it. It wasn't easy trying to avoid getting the white water onto her sword either, and her inconveniently long skirt made everything much harder. She bunched its fabric into one fist and quickly, panting, made her way through the water.

A sharp scream from above. Startled, she looked up. There were birds, or bats, black-red ones, flocking above. Streamlined bodies with gigantic wings, just three or four of them, but they seemed to cover the whole sky. The wings became more blood-crimson toward the tips. The sight of these bloodied-looking wings and the sound of their screams, or keening, that cut through the thick fog made her shudder.

The water began to grow deeper. It rose past her calves, her knees, and then wrapped around her thighs. She remembered too late the young man's gun she had strapped to her thigh, but she couldn't hold up the sword in one hand and unholster the gun with the other. Soon the dense white water came up past her stomach and chest, and she held up her sword high above her head with both hands. The thick fog had already been making it hard for her to breathe, but now the water felt like it was trying to squeeze out the breath from her lungs.

The fog lifted a little at the midpoint of the river. She observed the river was split clearly into two different currents. One current was the heavy water, which was milky and slow. But at the middle of the river where the fog lifted, the water suddenly became clear, so clear she could see the bottom of the river, the water not mixed at all with the heavy white fluid that she had come through.

Were these two different currents made of liquid that was different from that of Earth? Was it safe to be inside either one?

She looked about her carefully. She couldn't see behind her because of the fog, but in front of her she could see the people who had already crossed the river and were coming up onto the embankment on the other side.

Taking a deep breath, she took a cautious step into the clear-water part of the river.

Wisps of the white, opaque water followed her into the clear part but soon vanished in the flow. The water of the clear side felt lighter. Its side of the river was also much deeper, and she sank more into it the farther she got, but it was easier to maneuver in. The water went up from her chest to her chin. When the water hit her nose, she took a deep breath and plunged her face into the river.

When she opened her eyes in the water, she saw a white alien. Their eyes met.

The white alien was faster. They aimed the white wand in their hand toward her. She froze.

But then the white alien shook their head, as if warning her. Without taking their gaze off her, the white alien, still grasping their wand, swam to the edge of the river and disappeared out of the water.

For a long time, until she couldn't hold her breath any longer, she stood there in the water, completely still. And only when she couldn't stand it anymore, she peeked out of the water—the white alien was gone, and there were more of the Empire's prisoners on the embankment. The embankment was smooth and white, and the prisoners were having trouble trying to find handholds on its surface. There wasn't a single blade of grass or even a weed growing on the side of the clear water, and there weren't any natural-looking rocks or pebbles there, just artificial, smooth surfaces.

How the white alien had managed to come down the embankment without being seen by the other prisoners and how they could hold their breath for so long underwater were mysteries to her, but the more urgent matter was that she needed to warn the others that she had been seen by a patrolling white alien and they had gone to get reinforcements. She swam to the embankment as quickly as she could, crossing the expanse of clear flow.

The water became more shallow. Soaking wet, holding up her sword in its scabbard with her left hand and her skirt bunched in her right as she fought the water that tried to unravel it from her grasp, she walked as quickly as possible.

As soon as she came out of the water, the ground vibrated

again. There was a dull, deep sound. Like a sigh, or the wind being taken out of something, a fogged, low sound.

A white light flashed across the river surface. It directly hit one of the Empire's flying machines that were looking down on the prisoners from the other side of the river.

The vehicle exploded. Even through the white fog, the flashes of red and yellow light and the sound of the explosion were unmistakable. Fragments scattered to the ground, and its remaining half crashed into the fog, covering the riverbank with black smoke.

Time stopped. She could only stand on the smooth white embankment, watching the Empire's flying machine crash.

The ground vibrated again, and she snapped back to her senses.

Above the pure white embankment hovered a translucent white disk.

*

Her first instinct was to cross the river back to where she had come from. An instinct shared by everyone else as they leaped back into the water.

The translucent disk fired white rays of light at the people in the river.

The river that flowed half white and half clear soon turned red.

There was nowhere to run.

She knocked on the smooth, white embankment. It had looked hard as marble at first glance, but it wasn't actually that solid. Using the rocks on the riverbed, she smashed in some handholds and footholds and began to climb up the embankment's side.

When she had made it up to the top and put down her scabbard, the first thing that faced her was a giant white alien. A specimen at least twice as large as the last one she had encountered. The white alien grabbed her by the scruff of the neck, raised her up, and tossed her aside. She flew in an arc to the ground and rolled all over in the white dust. She lost her sword. Light flashed in her eyes and her head rang; she couldn't breathe.

She looked around for her sword. There was no way of knowing if the sword would have any effect on the white giant, but such complicated thoughts did not occur to her in that moment. The sword was her only weapon, a part of her body, her avatar. *My sword, where is my sword …*

She looked up, and the end of a white wand was aimed right at her face.

She stared helplessly up at the white giant. The white giant, expressionless, was about to press the wand.

Gunshots. They sounded like they were coming from far away, a dull sound. At the same time, a bullet grazed the neck of the white giant.

The white giant grabbed their neck and stumbled. Pure white liquid oozed from between their gloved fingers as they held their wound.

The white giant fell.

The older man came up to her and raised her to her feet.

"Pull yourself together!"

She mumbled, "My sword—"

"Stay here and you die!"

She didn't listen to him. She spotted her red scabbard by the body of the slain white giant. Half running, half crawling to it, she grabbed it.

When she turned, she saw the older man was trying to get the wand out of the giant's hand.

"That won't—"

Before she could finish her sentence, another white giant appeared from behind the older man. She jumped to the fallen white giant's side and grabbed the giant's hand that was still gripping the wand, held it up, and twisted. The white giant that had appeared behind the older man was hit by the ensuing white ray and fell.

The older man was trying to say something to her. She drew her sword and threw it down against the white alien's arm.

The steel blade hit something and chipped, the chip bouncing against her face. The white alien's arm remained intact.

Aiming his gun at the white alien's arm, the older man fired. The bullet lodged itself in the armor.

When he aimed his gun once more, she dropped her scabbard and sword and raised her arms. The man, who'd been ready to shoot, looked up at her quizzically. Her eyes darted at him and then at their surroundings; he looked around.

He slowly lowered his gun when he realized they were surrounded by white aliens.

The white aliens led them into an enclosure fenced with straight white planks. Inside sat other prisoners. The sight of Indigo

Skirt and Light Green Skirt sitting together made her feel relief and worry and despair at the same time. She wanted to sob but also wanted to smile with gladness. She closed her eyes and took a deep breath.

The white aliens had plucked a plank from the ground, shoved her and the older man inside the gap, and stuck the plank back into the ground and left. A somewhat shabby structure for a prisoner-of-war camp.

What were they going to do to them? It was a good thing they hadn't all been executed. The fact that they hadn't been dragged into the translucent disk, however, worried her. Were they going to wait until they were all inside the enclosure before killing them? She looked closely at the white planks. Just as she was about to poke one, one of the prisoners said, "Don't."

She looked back. An elderly man was shaking his head. He said in awkward Imperial, "Flashing, pain."

He slowly presented the palm of his hand. There were black burn marks on his middle and index fingers. The black burns were surrounded by painfully red flesh that hurt her even to look at.

Deflated, she took stock of her prison. The white surroundings gave them almost no option to do anything but wait.

And that's what she decided to do. She sat among the other prisoners, crouching down and covering her head with her arms.

After a little while, she began to doze.

She was woken by a murmur. The white aliens had opened a plank and sent in more prisoners. Just as they were about to close the plank once more, a young man had tried to resist. But just a touch of the plank's edge sent the man collapsing, foaming at the mouth. They shoved him into the gap and slammed the plank down and left once more.

She ripped a little off her skirt. She went up to the man and wiped the foam from his mouth.

"Why are you wearing such clothes to a war?"

Precise and fluent Imperial. She looked back. It was the older man who had saved her by slicing the white alien's neck with a bullet, the one who had asked her where her young man had gone. He looked irritated.

She didn't answer. She neatly rearranged her skirt and sat back down again.

The older man kept interrogating her in precise Imperial. "That skirt. Is that appropriate wear for battle?"

"It's what the Imperials made her wear," retorted Indigo Skirt, also in Imperial.

"The Imperials didn't send us here to do battle," added Light Green Skirt. "You men are the ones who're supposed to do the war, and we're supposed to open our legs to you and die later. Can't you see that?"

The older man opened his mouth to reply but hesitated. His countenance darkened, and he bowed his head.

"I am sorry."

She glanced at the fallen young man who had foamed at the mouth. He was still unconscious but foaming no more, and his eyes were closed and his breathing regular. She stood up and adjusted her skirt once more. Indigo Skirt gestured to her. She walked up to her and sat down by her side.

A heavy silence followed.

Red Sword

For a while, there were no new prisoners. It was mostly quiet outside, and there were occasional vibrations, with some faint, indiscernible sounds in the far distance.

"What's happened?" Indigo Skirt wondered aloud in Imperial. "Is everyone dead?"

Instead of answering, Light Green Skirt embraced Indigo Skirt tightly.

The sight of them reminded her of the young man. The sight of him being hit by the white ray and splitting in half, his left eye staring at her—she shuddered. She shook her head, trying to get rid of the image.

The gun the young man had given her was still strapped to her thigh. The river water must've ruined it, surely? Could a soaked gun fire? Did it even have bullets? It was frustrating to know so little about guns. If only she had her sword, then she would know what to do. *Where's my sword? Will I be able to find it if I ever get out of here? Will I die the moment I step out of here before I can even start looking? Maybe we'll be dragged to those white people's spaceship ...*

"Banners." This was spoken by the older man, who had been peering out a gap in the planks. "Lots of banners. No end to them! Coming our way!"

"What banners?" asked another man who spoke Imperial. "*Whose* banners?"

The older man shook his head, and the other man got up and peered out the gap as well. Soon, everyone inside the fencing was trying to get a vantage point, careful not to touch the planks.

They weren't banners. They were skirts. Women had taken off their long skirts, tied them to their scabbards, and were holding them up like banners. The dim fog was cut through with white light, and through orange and red flames were women and men in the Empire's uniforms carrying the Empire's weapons, holding up colored skirts like banners and advancing toward them.

"The unnis," she whispered in her language, using the word for "older sister."

Indigo Skirt and Light Green Skirt came up to where she stood. Together, they stared out the narrow gap between the planks. They said nothing but gripped each other's hands, hard.

Prisoners were just prisoners. Until now, they each had their own burdens and each walked slowly toward their own deaths. Never had they thought of each other as "our side" or the possibility of being an "us."

But our side is coming now.

To save us.

Staring at the approach of the colorful banners, she found herself thinking these same two thoughts over and over.

The plank fence groaned as it fell. A woman wearing a gray Empire uniform reached out to the women and shouted, "Everybody out! Hurry!"

The prisoners readily complied. She noticed a large bloodstain in the back of her rescuer's uniform.

"Blood …"

The woman in the gray uniform frowned.

"It's from one of the crashed air vehicles, I took it off the back of a dead Imperial." Her tone turned matter of fact. "You better hurry, we can't keep back the white monsters for too long."

Red Sword

She ran toward the phalanx of people who wore the gray uniform of the Empire but were on her side. But she stopped near the spot where the older man had felled the white giant and quickly looked around for her sword.

"What are you doing!" shouted the woman in the gray uniform.

"My sword!" she shouted back.

A glimmer of red by the white giant. She almost fell as she threw herself upon her scabbard.

The moment she did, white light flashed over her head. A heat behind her ears and a smell of burning hair.

White aliens were massing from behind. As their thickly protected feet stomped the ground, the earth shook.

She searched for the white wand in the hand of the giant. But it was gone. Getting frantic, she searched about the giant's body. There was a larger and thicker wand holstered on the giant's hip. She placed it into the hand of the giant, wrapped her hands around their dead digits, aimed at the charging white aliens, and screwed her eyes shut.

The wand vibrated and a blinding-white ray burst forth. She opened her eyes a little and tried as best she could to aim, moving and squeezing the dead giant's hand with all her might. A large ray of incredibly pure whiteness crossed the air into the massing white aliens, and the recoil of the firing wand made her almost fall on her behind.

One of the white aliens flew into the air as the ray bounced off their armor and see-through helmet. Their chest armor had no trace of being hit, but there was a small black hole on their helmet visor with a crack growing out of it. The white alien, with some awkwardness, got back on their feet. The mass of white aliens paused as they watched the fallen one regain their footing, and they began moving again.

Gunshots. The white alien that had been hit by the ray fell backwards.

She looked back. The older man stood there, gun in hand.

"It's the helmet!" he shouted.

She quickly went back to aiming and firing with the dead giant's hand and wand, a gunshot following her every shot. White ray, gunshot. White ray, gunshot.

Only when every white alien had been felled did she realize the older man had managed to shoot them through the cracks in their helmets or armor once she had fired her ray upon them.

This made her determined to learn how to shoot.

The older man didn't make a run for it. Instead, he ran to the fallen white aliens. She followed, not knowing what he was about to do. He was trying to take the wands out of their dead hands.

"Glove, hand, without them, no!" she shouted in her inadequate Imperial. The older man didn't listen to her. He was busy rummaging through the belongings of the white aliens, finding other weapons and equipment.

One of the white aliens stirred and tried to get up. The moment she was about to scream, there was a gunshot. Once, then again. The first shot lodged itself in the barrel of the white alien's wand while the second pierced the white alien in the neck. The white alien stopped moving.

The elderly man from inside the fence appeared next to her, holding a gun in his left hand as his right was injured.

"You are ruining the weapons!" the rummaging man shouted in anger.

"You fool," shouted back the elderly man. "You can't operate any of those weapons without the right biometric information! You've got to run instead!"

She grabbed the hand of a nearby white alien holding a wand and squeezed the grip. A white ray appeared. She dragged the body by the arm, and using the ray like a sword, she severed the wrist of the next white alien. She gave the hand to the rummaging man.

Meanwhile, the old man behind her stared at her, his mouth agape. He quickly turned and ran away.

The other man carefully accepted the white alien's hand. He shook it so the hand inside the glove slipped out. Swiftly, he grabbed as many white wands and other equipment as he could.

"Let's go," he said.

Grasping her red sword close to her chest, she ran beside the older man.

They arrived at the embankment. Right before they could slide down its porcelain-smooth walls into the water, the ground vibrated.

She looked back. White aliens, aiming their wands towards her and her friends.

The ground vibrated again, threatening. The vibrations grew stronger and stronger. A side of the gray sky began to darken.

All the white aliens turned their heads in the same direction. Following their gaze, she turned as well.

A black, gigantic bird-like animal flew up from afar.

As she stared in shock, the animal spread its wings, seemingly covering the whole sky. The ground vibrated so much that she felt dizzy. The atmosphere itself seemed to shake. The gigantic animal opened its mouth and vomited a black-red liquid that sprayed out into the air. Breathing in even a tiny droplet made the nose and throat burn, and a drop on the skin created rashes and pustules. Any that got in the eyes caused blindness and constant tears. Even the white aliens wrapped in their armor took shelter, trying to shake off any droplets that came on them.

"Run!" shouted the unknown woman in the gray uniform to her.

She ran along the embankment and slid down into the clear river water.

The red-black liquid changed to blood-red on the surface of the water and floated like oil. Some of it sank and touched her back and shoulder. This was how she learned, through an agony of pain, that her shoulder wound from yesterday still hadn't healed. It was like fire running down her shoulder and back. Gritting her teeth, she swam deeper into the water. She was half-afraid of dropping her sword or losing the gun holstered to her thigh, but now was not the time to worry about her weapons.

She came upon the flowing white water on the other half of the river. Underwater, the sight of that wall-like whiteness seemed even stranger. Hesitant at first, her lungs began burning so much that she hurriedly swam into the opaque whiteness.

Everything was white around her—she could see nothing else—but the vibrations were nevertheless felt even in immersion. Had the black animal followed her into the fog? When she surfaced, would she become covered in the mysterious black-red substance it vomited and sizzle to death? Or would she be made prisoner again by the white aliens? What if everyone she had known was dead?

She surfaced. The riverbank, awash in fog.

A deep breath. The air, once so tepid and unpleasant, seemed sweet to her now. Gratefully, she kept breathing in until a water droplet caught in her throat, and she began to cough violently, bending over in the effort.

Once she could breathe properly again, she came out onto the riverbank. The fog existed only on this side, as if cut by a knife along the demarcation in the water, which made the other side relatively clear enough to see. The large animal was like a bat or bird. It was spewing its red-black liquid, attacking the white disk of the white aliens. The white aliens fought back with their rays.

"The birds are fighting our battle for us …"

She turned at the voice. Indigo Skirt stood near her. She was about to ask after Light Green Skirt but stopped herself.

As the two women watched, the white aliens fired white light on the black bird. The black bird faltered when hit, but then would get back up and spew its bloody liquid again, making the earth and sky shake with its cries—then, it suddenly flew away.

"They come," said Indigo Skirt.

The white aliens' disk rose slowly to the sky. The ones who didn't make it to the disk made large strides as if stepping on air to descend the embankment and disappear into the water. At first it seemed they sank, but in the next moment, their heads resurfaced at a surprisingly close distance as they rapidly made their way across the water. The water suddenly filled with bobbing white aliens on their way to where they stood by the opaque water.

She unsheathed her sword. She held it in her left hand, her scabbard in her right.

Indigo Skirt also brought out a small indigo scabbard. The sword that came out of it was wide and short. Indigo Skirt held it firm in her right hand.

"Too short, right?" Indigo Skirt said to her.

She grinned in answer.

By the time the white aliens were close enough for such a short sword to be effective, they would already be dead …

She thought of her own chipped blade. She gripped the sword hilt with all her strength.

*

"Duck!"

As she was about to turn at the sharp sound of a female voice, Indigo Skirt grabbed her collar and dragged her to the ground. The two of them fell flat upon the white dust.

Something loud flew over their heads and exploded over the river. Twice.

The white water became even whiter. The broken body parts of the white aliens floated past them.

"Fire!"

She ducked again, protecting her head. The loud and fast things, for the third time, exploded over the river.

As they looked behind them, they saw Light Green Skirt

holding up a large cylinder on her shoulder. Light Green Skirt noticed Indigo Skirt and winked at her. Then, she put down her cylinder and tossed a gun to both Indigo Skirt and her.

"How did you fire that?" shouted Indigo Skirt. "I thought you needed biometric information to use it?"

"The security chips broke when the vehicle was shot by those white aliens." Light Green Skirt patted the cylinder next to her and picked up a long rifle. "As for the unbroken ones, we smashed them." Tossing her head back, she pointed to her own neck. "Shoot at them here. Their other parts are covered in metal casing, it's a waste of bullets."

And so, she sheathed her sword and picked up a gun for the first time. Right next to the trigger, where the thumb would rest, a crack revealed part of the bullet chamber inside.

From the thick white water, the surviving white aliens started to drag themselves out of the river like ghosts.

She held up her gun. She aimed for right below their helmets.

The battle wasn't long. Or perhaps it was. She had no way of knowing.

Just as she had no way of knowing the recoil from the gun would be so strong. The first bullet ricocheted off a white alien's helmet, and the recoil made her fall backward and drop her gun. The white alien walked right up to her, and she grabbed whatever was around her and threw it.

The white alien deftly avoided it. The barrel of their white wand was aiming at her when she unsheathed her sword and thrust her blade. Her intention was to split the barrel of the wand, but instead, her sword caught the bottom of the barrel and pushed it upward, knocking the wand out of the white alien's hand, the ray flying off into the sky.

Which gave her just enough time to grab the gun she had dropped and stand up. As she was about to aim at the white alien, they jumped on her.

She was crushed underneath. The white alien was wearing a thick metal armor that covered their entire body. It was very different from the hard but thin armor the female white alien had worn in her first encounter with the white aliens. She struggled to move under the weight.

A good thing was that the white alien was much larger than she was, and the armor perhaps *too* thick. They tried to strangle her or attack her head, but she was too small and the white alien too large, crushing her under one shoulder as they tried and failed to grab her with their free arm.

Shoot at them here.

She suddenly remembered Light Green Skirt pointing at her neck. She angled her hand the best she could, but her arm being caught in the white alien's armpit, she couldn't quite aim at the neck.

Anyway—she fired. Once, twice, thrice, continuing, until there were no more bullets in the magazine.

The white alien crushing her stopped moving.

With all her might, she managed to get herself out from underneath the hunk of metal, lifting the wall-like arm a tiny bit and throwing it aside so the rest of the body would roll away. Her skirt, still wedged underneath the white alien's armor, tore as she tried to dislodge herself.

Finally, she got up and inspected the corpse. Most of the

bullets seemed to have glanced off the back of the white alien's armor. But miraculously enough, a few shots seemed to have found their way into the neck. There was a small gap between the helmet and the body armor, and white liquid flowed from it.

She quickly found her sword and sheathed it in her scabbard. She also grabbed the white alien's wand.

And she ran. She had to get away from this river as fast as possible.

She wanted to live. She didn't go as far as to think so in so many words, but she wanted, desperately, to live.

Someone grabbed her. With a scream, she tried to wrench herself free, but the grip on her got stronger.

"Calm down. Stop that."

She looked up. It was the older man. She stopped struggling.

"Look over there."

He gestured with his chin. She looked.

The flying vehicle of the Empire. It circled overhead at a low altitude.

"I thought it crashed?" she murmured, confused.

"It's a different one," the man said, "sent out later on. If you run now, you'll die by the hand of the Imperials."

She stared at the vehicle. After a long time, she nodded. The man let her go.

She handed him the wand procured from the white alien and the gun Light Green Skirt had given her. The man looked at her askance.

"This, you wanted," she said in her awkward Imperial. Lifting the gun a bit, she added, "This, I don't know how."

The man smiled a little. A glimpse of healthy white teeth.

The smile was a slight shock to her. It had been a long time since she'd seen someone smile, or seen any white that wasn't the ominous and ashy white of this planet. It felt like the first time she was seeing such a thing in her life.

*

The Imperials landed. From the patrol ship came out the cruel gray uniforms. They threatened her, the man, and the other surviving prisoners with guns. The man's guns and wand given by her were confiscated. Her red scabbard and the sword inside it were confiscated. And the Imperials, upon glimpsing through her torn skirt the young man's gun holstered on her thigh, slapped her and struck her head before confiscating that, too.

The men and women were taken inside the patrol ship and divided from each other and thrown into separate cells. The prisoners who had put on the gray uniforms had their uniforms taken from them and were beaten. She aided these beaten and bleeding women when they were thrown into their room with them, watching over them all night with Indigo Skirt and Light Green Skirt.

"Tumina." This was what Indigo Skirt whispered to her in between wiping the blood from the injured women and holding their hands and telling them it's all right, it'll be all right. "My name is Tumina." Tumina tilted her head in Light Green Skirt's direction. "And that's Atung."

She told them her name as well.

Tumina and Atung solemnly nodded and said nothing. They

went back to taking care of their injured friends.

Her stomach growled. She realized she was famished. Her last meal was a distant memory. Muttering under her breath that she was hungry, she quickly silenced herself in case Tumina or Atung or any of the other starving prisoners should hear.

Someone tapped her shoulder.

"You're hungry?"

She looked back. There stood a woman wearing a purple skirt.

She knew this woman. Every prisoner in the ship knew her.

Isfobeddin. All the women depended on her and kept her at an arm's length at the same time.

"Should I get you some food?" she said with a smile. It chilled her.

She shook her head.

Another smile. "Wait a little."

Isfobeddin slipped out the door like it was nothing.

That was who she was. While everyone else was beaten and imprisoned, Isfobeddin could slip out unhindered by the Imperial standing guard with a rifle and go anywhere she chose.

The prisoner who had her salvaged uniform taken from her and beaten for it tried to talk. She hushed her.

"It's all right. Don't speak. Yes, lie down again, try to rest—"

"Have some."

She almost jumped out of her skin. Isfobeddin was like a cat. She moved without a sound and smiled that terrifying smile at everyone.

There it was again.

"A gift. For fighting so well today."

She hesitated. Isfobeddin smiled widely. She left a small

bundle by her and, just as silently as she had come, disappeared somewhere.

She didn't touch the bundle. Touching it might conjure up Isfobeddin again. Who knew what price she would ask for this bundle, and whether it would be a price she could pay.

Indigo Skirt, or Tumina, reached out and picked up the bundle before anything could be said.

Light Green Skirt, Atung, took the water bottle Tumina handed her and slowly dripped some of its contents onto an injured prisoner's lips. She also crumbed a handful of emergency rations from the bundle and placed it in her mouth.

"You should drink, too." Tumina held out the bottle.

As she hesitated, Atung interjected, "You've already taken it from her. Whatever happens next, it's better to face it a little less hungry and thirsty."

She acquiesced. She took the bottle from Tumina.

The water was sweet. Carefully, in order to not accidentally drink the whole bottle, she drank the cold water little by little, savoring it as it trickled down her throat.

After her drink, and eating some of the crumbs Atung had handed her, she went back to looking after the other prisoners. Only when the injured were all settled and her companions laid down to rest themselves did she find a corner to curl up in. She nodded off.

A feeling of something cold and hard creeping into her chest made her wake up with a start.

The young man was standing right before her eyes.

—Don't die.

It was his voice.

—I love you.

The young man disappeared.

She tried to follow him. She tried to get up and call out his name. But her body refused to move. She tried with all her might, and woke up once more.

In her embrace was the young man's gun. She had crossed the opaque and clear river twice with it, but it wasn't waterlogged or broken. Just as it had been when the young man had given it to her for the first time, the gun was cold and dry and hard and gleamed with reassuring promise.

She smiled. Hugging the gun close to her, she fell back into the deep sleep of the exhausted and hungry.

3. *Isfobeddin*

"So what do you want from me?"

Isfobeddin asked this question as she looked upon the older man. The man was surprised.

He had never said he'd wanted anything. All he had been doing was staring at the woman, who had come into the men's prison as if she lived there and was now whispering with someone in the corner.

"Tell me what you want," Isfobeddin said once more.

And she smiled. A cat-like smile, revealing two canines. The smile of a carnivore.

He swallowed and gathered his strength.

"Where are the guns, ma'am? The weapons we stole from the white aliens."

"What will you give me if I tell you?"

He didn't know what to say. There was nothing he could give to Isfobeddin. It had never occurred to him to do an exchange or barter when he first spoke to her. He fell silent.

But Isfobeddin, after a long look, made that cat-like smile again, the edges of her mouth curling up to reveal her teeth.

"Follow me," she said, raising her right hand and gesturing lightly to the door.

This was even more disconcerting. The door was locked. Follow her? To where? How?

Isfobeddin walked up to the door and knocked on it a few times. It opened smoothly as if it had never been locked.

She made another gesture. The man stood and followed her.

The corridor was narrow, long, and dark. The floor was scattered with all sorts of things, and the wall was occasionally sticky and stank of something. Isfobeddin walked through the belly of the Imperials' ship with the ease of someone who owned the place.

At the end of a hall, Isfobeddin suddenly disappeared. The man panicked, looking around—from the darkness, her face emerged, her cat-like smile in place. She gestured once more. The man followed that gesture into a door on the left. Behind him, the door slammed shut, and the sound of a heavy bolt being slid echoed in his ears.

Isfobeddin was quick. With a practiced air, she lowered the man's trousers and gripped his genitals in her hand. As the man opened his mouth in surprise, Isfobeddin wrapped both hands around his extremities and grasped them hard, silencing him. She rubbed quickly and slid something thin and slick and stretchy over his member. Before the man could speak, her hand, then her lips, stopped his mouth from speaking. Something warm and damp covered the man.

The man realized he had to make a decision. Either he wrested himself away from Isfobeddin or give her what she wanted. But if he threw her off now, he would never get the information he wanted. And somehow he knew that getting on this woman's bad side would not end well for him down the line. He didn't know what kind of person she was. But anyone who could go in and out of holding cells full of prisoners with no resistance could be no ordinary prisoner.

So he let himself relax. Instead of grasping her waist and throwing Isfobeddin from him, his hands found the wall behind his back and held his body steady.

In the empty darkness of the room, the only sound they could hear was their low, rough breathing.

After a climax that was closer to shock than exhilaration, Isfobeddin, with the same deftness and speed in which she had started, took the thin and stretching thing from his member and fixed his trousers. She put something cold and hard in the man's hand, gave him a kiss on the lips, and whispered, "Good job."

Isfobeddin went out the door.

The man grasped the hard object she had given him. He couldn't see it in the dark, but it was easy enough to tell it was the wand he had stolen from the white aliens. Which was why he quickly went out of the room and hissed at the disappearing Isfobeddin's back, "I can't do anything with this! I need the biometric trigger!"

"That's your problem," she said to the corridor wall without even looking at him. In the next moment, she vanished into the dark.

As soon as he got out of the corridor, he was captured by the Imperials, who threw him back into the men's cell. Even as he was tossed and was rolling on the cell floor, he took care not to let on that there was a wand hidden in his clothes. His head hit a wall, and he felt dazed. But as he rubbed his head and shoulder, his other hand never let go of the wand under his jacket.

All night, he stared at the white wand. The other men, knowing he had come back from a tryst with Isfobeddin, mocked him with their stifled laughter or made hostile eyes at him. The man didn't care. He stared at the wand and wondered how this weapon could be used. Eventually, he tucked it into his tunic and fell asleep. He was awoken in the morning when someone grabbed him by the scruff of the neck. As he was being dragged out of the ship, he hastily made sure the wand was still underneath his clothes.

"I got this."

The older man had found her as they were being marched through the planet's surface again and gave her a glimpse of the end of the white wand. She looked back at him with a dispassionate, pale face.

"Isfobeddin?"

The man had a sudden memory of Isfobeddin's lips locking on his, her almost uninterestedly efficient hands working on his genitals. The shame made him unable to reply.

"That person, be careful ..." she murmured, sighing. She said no more and continued to walk on, mechanical and expressionless.

The man didn't know what to make of this. He still felt shame, but he was afraid she would walk away from him forever, so he quickly caught up to her again.

"Why?"

She pretended not to hear. The man persisted.

"What do you know of her?"

She turned her head to look at him. Her eyes were bloodshot and vacant.

The man explained, "You know, of that Is ... Isfo ..." He couldn't remember her exact name.

She, reluctantly, opened her exhausted mouth to speak. "Stolen. Her children."

The man couldn't understand at first.

"Children ... stolen? By the Imperials?"

She nodded. "Two. Child-male, child-female."

"A son and a daughter?"

She nodded, still looking tired.

"Are they dead?" the man asked again.

She shook her head. "Don't know."

Every woman knew this story. That one must never interfere with a mother whose child was stolen, that a mother would do anything to find her child. That's what the women said to each other. And so, while they mostly feared and sometimes abhorred Isfobeddin, they pitied her as well.

Someone had carefully said that it would've been better if the children had been killed. But Isfobeddin had told them the last time she had seen her children, they were alive. That while the Imperials took her little son and daughter kicking and screaming, they had not killed them. If anything, they seemed to be taking care not to hurt them as they dragged them away. At least, that was what Isfobeddin remembered. She believed her children were still alive. And this belief trapped her in a prison better guarded than any other in the Empire, as her children would be eternal hostages. Isfobeddin traded in information in order to find out what had happened to her children, and the other prisoners were able to get what they needed and wanted thanks to this, but more often than not, they ended up worse off. It was assumed that the reason the prisoners who had raided the flying vehicle for Imperial weapons had been found out, and the fact that they had all been thrown in lockup despite winning a battle, was because of Isfobeddin.

She was too tired to explain all this to the man. Which was why when he tried to ask her more questions, she listlessly shook her head.

Exhausted and hungry, her wounds on her shoulder and leg and wrist throbbing with pain, she was thinking about whetstones. Her skirt, which had reached her ankles, had been torn during the battle of the day before, so she left just enough length on it to conceal the gun the young man had given her and tore off a part that kept getting in her way. Her scabbard now knocked against her bare leg every time she took a step. She was thinking of the sword in that scabbard. If she wanted to repair the chip in it, she either needed to make a new blade or fill in the chip somehow. For which she would need a blacksmith. But here in this place, in this situation, it would be impossible to get a new blade or repair her old one. The best she could do was to use a whetstone to sharpen the blade and get the chip out as much as possible.

And to do that, she needed a whetstone. How was she to procure one here?

Isfobeddin?

She found herself shaking her head.

"How do you know these things?" the man said. "Do the women speak of such things among themselves?"

She looked back at him askance. Her head was so full of whetstones and such that it took a moment for her to realize the man was talking about Isfobeddin.

"Why not know?" she said, answering with a question. "Together, six years, long time?"

"Six years?" The man looked puzzled.

They didn't get a chance to continue. Through the dense clouds in the sky, a white vessel, exactly the same white as the clouds, appeared without a sound. It began firing rays at the prisoners, who were marching to the white and clear river from the day before.

The prisoners screamed and scattered.

She began to run. Not knowing where to go, she simply began to run away from the ship as fast as she could.

She stumbled on something. She was surrounded by fog and overwhelmed by fear, which meant she hadn't noticed she'd been running directly to the river from yesterday.

She tried to dislodge what had made her stumble. Sticky and thin but tenacious blades of grass came into her grasp. The fog was especially thick at the riverbank, and she couldn't see her own feet. But she frantically tried to disentangle her feet from the grass as best she could.

A strong hand grabbed her wrist. Through the translucent visor of a white helmet, she met the yellow eyes of a white face.

In the next moment, she was being dragged by the yellow-eyed white alien into the foggy water.

Underwater, she was surrounded by white and couldn't breathe. She could barely understand what happened next.

The yellow-eyed white alien tried to point their wand at her. She quickly took out her scabbard and struck the white alien's wrist with it. The white alien dropped their wand, which disappeared into the depths.

The white alien then tried to grab her with both hands. And a third arm, a mechanical one protruding from the white alien's back, grabbed at her as well.

The mechanical arm snatched the scabbard from her hand. As she fought to get it back, the white alien slapped her, hard. She was hit right on the temple. Almost blacking out, she slowly spun in the water before sinking, headfirst, into the deeper water.

She contemplated the murky white depths, flailing a little as she tried not to sink. Something caught her hand. She grabbed it with all her might.

It was the boot of the white alien. They shook their foot to get her off, but she held on fast. She was out of breath and everything before her was white, and not a single thought entered her mind. She was running on pure instinct.

She felt a slight protrusion on the boot of the white alien. With all her might, she pinched it. The white alien once more tried to kick her off their foot.

The boot came off. Something was dropped into the water, a black object in the murky white.

She grabbed it. There was a bumpy part. She squeezed it in her fist as hard as she could.

The white alien's mechanical arm let go of her sword.

Red Sword

The white alien tried to grab their mechanical arm and shake her off at the same time. But they were half-submerged, and their movements were slow. She avoided the kicks and twisted the black device in her hand this way and that. The mechanical arm moved in response to her manipulation of the device.

She tried pushing the device forward.

The arm grabbed the white alien's translucent helmet.

She twisted the device.

The mechanical arm pierced the helmet. The white alien went into spasms, their foot still in her grasp.

The white liquid flowing out of the white alien's helmet made the white river water even whiter. Life quickly seeped out of their yellow eyes, now fully revealed.

Even after the white alien had stopped flailing, she held onto the black device for as long as her breath would allow.

The scabbard the mechanical arm had dropped floated to her side. She let go of the device and grabbed the scabbard. Leaving the dead white alien to sink, she began to swim up to the surface.

It was easier said than done. Her underwater struggle with the white alien had flipped her so many times that she didn't know where was up anymore, and she didn't know which way to swim. No matter how much she swam in whichever direction, there was only more white, and she felt no closer to the surface.

She needed to breathe. She needed to breathe *now*. Fear struck her every cell.

Flailing around in a panic made her more desperate for breath. The more desperate, the more fear rose in her, and the less she could see in front of her or think straight.

She began moving in a random direction, holding up the scabbard in front of her. Maybe someone would see its red in the white fog. But she couldn't tell if she were holding the scabbard toward the surface or the depths.

She needed to breathe in the next few seconds or she'd die. As she opened her mouth to breathe, the white water gagged her.

She lost consciousness.

The man had tried to follow her but lost her. She had fallen and therefore slipped out of sight, and when he tried to follow her screams, he was surrounded by white aliens.

The man whipped out the white wand he had hidden in his clothing. He knew, of course, that he couldn't use it. But maybe the white aliens didn't know that. The white aliens tensed up when they saw his weapon, and his confident handling of it made them take a step back. The man desperately tried to think of a way to escape as he slowly retreated backward.

But one of the white aliens called his bluff and unholstered their wand and fired at the man. The man leaped to the side to avoid the ray and fell to the ground.

The white aliens rushed him. If just one of them had managed to accurately fire at him on the ground, he would've died instantly. But the white aliens were too nervous from his feint and indiscriminate in their firing, which allowed him to twist this way and that, avoiding their fire. He was grazed here and there with burns, but he had no time to feel pain.

One of the white aliens tried to stamp down on his face. The man rolled away just in time, and he struck the wand down as hard as he could on the white alien's foot.

Nothing happened to the white alien's foot. Instead, a white ray issued forth from the man's wand, piercing upward. The ray hit the white alien's neck, and the man fell backward.

The man wasted only half a second realizing what had just happened. He grabbed the white alien's foot again and made the side of the wand touch the armor as he started firing at the advancing white aliens.

When all the white aliens had fallen, the man slowly got up. His limbs were bloodied, and his right hip throbbed with pain. He hoisted up his ripped tunic to see the damage. From his hip to his armpit was a black line where a ray had grazed him. The man grimaced and gritted his teeth.

He holstered his wand onto his waistband and pulled off the gloves of the white alien fallen next to him. After putting them on, he unhooked the larger, thicker wand the white alien had at their side and holstered that as well. He got up and looked around, seeing if any other enemies were approaching. He saw, then, in the distance, a red spot in the surrounding white.

Her. It was her sword.

The man jumped into the white river.

She had been dragged into the middle of the white strand of the two-stranded river. Avoiding the battle on the foggy side, the man dragged her to the clear side and pulled her up to shore.

She wasn't breathing. He didn't know what to do. He shook

her, knocked on her back, rubbed it, and raised her arms and pressed down on her stomach and chest.

That did the trick. She spurted white water, and the man turned her on her side so she could vomit easier. After a long while of vomiting and coughing, she lay down on her back.

This frightened the man. He shook her.

"Do not ..."

Her voice was weak, but it was enough to reassure the man.

"My sword ..."

The man grabbed the red scabbard and placed it in her grasp. She smiled weakly, reassured, and closed her eyes. This scared him once more.

"Wake up!" he shouted.

She opened her eyes again.

"Feet ..." she mumbled. The man brought his ear to her mouth to hear what she was saying.

She spoke of the black device inside the white alien's boot and how moving or twisting or pressing or tilting it could control the third arm on their backs.

The man nodded. He then told her about the wands working when contact was made not only with their gloves but with their boots.

She closed her eyes and opened them again. With great effort, and with support from the man, she sat up.

She gripped the scabbard of her sword and smashed some handholds and footholds into the smooth embankment next to the gravelly shore and began climbing to the other side, the man following her, ready to catch her if she fell.

Near the top of the embankment, she carefully peered over the edge to take in the situation on the other side. There was the translucent white disk she had seen before. But no white aliens surrounding it this time.

Before she made it over the embankment, the man handed her one of the gloves he was wearing and a white wand. She put on the glove and took the wand in her hand. The glove was big on her, and she had to grip the wand hard not to drop it.

Carefully, she made her way over the embankment. The man followed.

They hadn't gone three steps before they were surrounded by white aliens.

They took back the gloves and wands first. But despite their expectations, the white aliens didn't then immediately kill or maim them. Instead, they were made to walk with them to the white disk. As they made their way, she spotted from the corner of her eye some familiar faces hiding by the embankment on this side. One of those faces was Isfobeddin's.

The disk was perfectly round and smooth, and it was impossible to tell where the front was and where was the back. The two prisoners stopped when they were made to. A split appeared on the surface of the disk, and a passageway slowly descended to where they stood. The prisoners and white aliens entered it, and the passageway began to slowly retract back into the ship.

They were walked down the white corridors. The ceiling and floor and walls were covered with machines and screens, some that resembled those of the Imperials they were familiar with, but others that were completely inscrutable in their use. As they looked around vigorously at their surroundings, the white aliens turned aggressive and blocked their views from the side with their bodies.

As she let herself be led, it occurred to her that the inside of the white spaceship was eerily quiet. There was the whirring and clicking of various machinery and panels, the low vibrations of an engine or motor, and other sounds one might expect to hear in the interior of a spaceship. In that sense, at least, it resembled the Imperial patrol ship.

But almost no human voices could be heard. No shouted orders, no warnings being blared on speakers. The white aliens occasionally saluted each other by raising their hands when they passed one another, but never spoke. The ones who had taken their helmets off had pale, sometimes blue faces, with others occasionally reddish, with eyes and hair that ranged from light gray to yellow, green, blue, and light brown, but not a single one of them opened their mouths to speak.

The floor vibrated, almost an earthquake. All the white aliens stopped in their tracks. In her surprise, she had stumbled, but even before the man could help her, one of the white aliens roughly grabbed her arm and righted her.

A white wall next to them opened, revealing a white alien standing inside a recess. They looked somewhat female, but it was generally difficult to tell what the genders of the white aliens were. This thin, old white alien seemed to be in some sort of high position. The others all raised their hands in salute, and the thin, old female white alien raised her hand in return. She then sat down in her seat in the recess and switched on various devices.

—Hoooow-have-you-come-come-to-in-in-vade-our-rrr-planet?

A machine voice was speaking Imperial. It sounded like an inventor who didn't know what language sounded like had used a machine to make consonants and vowels separately and mashed them together any which way. It sounded foreign, almost incomprehensible, and monstrous.

Neither of them answered at first. They didn't know what to say. The machine spoke again.

—Wh-aat-iss-your-purp-osse?... Reureureu-ratya-is-it?

Daunted, she turned to the man. The man looked back at her, also at a loss. Neither of them had understood that last word. The white aliens seemed to not process liquid consonants properly.

"We are prisoners!" she shouted. "Our purpose is freedom! The Imperials made us fight. If we win, we are free."

—Prrrrrrisoner?

The machine voice of the thin and old white alien seemed to brood over her answer with a question. Then, the white alien took out another device that was connected to the voice device and pressed the buttons on it, looking down at its output.

—Prrrrisoner-then-prrrrrisoner-of-warrr?

The white alien didn't wait for an answer.

—For-threeee-centurieeeees-barrrrli-agh-empirrre-never-warr-rrred-with-settlerrrrsss.

"No!" shouted the man. "Your information is wrong! We lost our nation, our homeland! We are not invading this planet because we want to!"

A light vibration surrounded them. In the next moment, one of the white guards slapped the man hard in the back of the head. When he fell, another white alien grabbed him like some inanimate object and propped him up so he would stand.

—Ba-rrrrrr-lia-gh-empirrrrre-soldierssss-will-beeee-executeeeeed-wheeeen-thee-fooog-liftsssss.

The declaration was final.

The man tried to speak, but even before the vibrations happened, a white alien struck the man's sternum with their wand. The man fell, the other white alien still holding him by the scruff of the neck. She said nothing.

The thin, old white alien turned off her devices one by one. The floor vibrated again. When it ceased, all the white aliens saluted. When she saluted back, the wall of the recess slid shut.

The fog seemed to lift for a moment, but then it began to rain. The drops were large, white, cold, and heavy, and left traces of white where they fell on clothes and skin. The taste of the rain, when the droplets slipped into the prisoners' mouths, was dusty and gag-inducing. The white aliens stood in the rain, their helmet visors covered in white drops, watching them.

They were both standing on top of the embankment, their hands tied behind their backs, getting drenched in the rain. She was breathing heavily. The soaking rain was giving her chills, and the white air and dust-tasting raindrops were making it harder for her to breathe.

"Take slow breaths," the man advised her. "Inhale, exhale. Good, like that."

"Why not kill us now?" she asked, panting.

"They're waiting for the rain to stop," the man whispered, "so the people across the river can see."

Red Sword

The people across the river. How many of them would be left now, after the way the white spaceship had fired its rays? What had become of Indigo Skirt and Light Green Skirt? And of the women they had been locked up with all night?

The rain began to fall even harder. The thick drops hurt her back as they thudded on her, and the humidity was making breathing so difficult that she was panting like a fish that had pushed its snout through the surface and was desperately taking in air. Strands of rain speared the ground, making the white earth tremble.

Through that tremor came gunshots. The heads of the white aliens swiveled as one toward the source. Through the falling white strands emerged gray shadows.

"Duck!" the man shouted as he kicked her ankle. Their hands still tied behind her back, they fell from the low embankment to the ground, facedown. She couldn't see anything, but she couldn't complain as something salty flowed from her nose and lips into her mouth. Bullets were flying over her head and also making the ground around her splatter.

She crawled. She didn't know where she was going, but it had to be somewhere she could avoid the bullets and untie herself. As she crawled through the white mud, dragging her bloody face, she suddenly felt her hands become free.

Indigo Skirt helped her to her feet. She then handed her a glove and white wand she had taken from a fallen white alien. Before she could thank her, Indigo Skirt turned and ran with the other prisoners toward the white spaceship.

"Don't fire your guns!" shouted Isfobeddin when they were met with a phalanx of white aliens who had come out of the ship to fight them. "The spaceship is a trophy of war! We cannot damage it!"

"What nonsense. How can we fight without our guns?" shouted back a man standing nearby. As the advancing white aliens raised their wands, the man who had shouted raised his gun to fire.

A gray-uniformed Imperial standing behind the prisoners fired at the aiming man. He screamed as he dropped to the ground.

Neither the white aliens nor the prisoners understood what had just happened. When a prisoner finally came to their senses and tried to run from the spaceship, screaming, the gray uniforms were quicker. The prisoner was shot in the back.

"Do not fire. Repeat. Do not fire." The commanding gray uniform added, "Attack!"

The prisoners looked at each other. They were stuck between the Imperials and the white aliens. As they hesitated, the gray uniforms took a step closer.

"No choice, then," said a man standing in front of her. He dropped his gun. The others dropped their guns.

And the white aliens, reassured, lowered their wands as well.

But the women stepped forward, swords drawn.

And the men, using only their bare hands, attacked.

It was not a fair fight. The women's swords broke and warped. The prisoners fell, hit by white rays. If they tried to run, the gray uniforms behind them shot them.

Red Sword

When a white alien in front of her raised their wand, she grabbed their wrist and tried to redirect the ray, but fell to the ground when she was hit by another white alien. Something hard pressed down on the back of her head. She swung wide her chipped and broken blade, but something hit her wrist and she dropped her sword. She could not get up.

Strapped to her thigh still was the young man's gun. Still prone, she brought her hand to her leg to get it out.

In that moment, someone fell right next to her.

The man. The older man who was somehow always by her side since she arrived on the white planet, the man who had saved her from drowning in the river, who now had an Imperial bullet that had been meant for her through his neck instead. The man's blood splattered on her face. His mouth was open in a silent scream, eyes still wide in surprise.

She screamed. Whether it was from anger or fear, she couldn't say. She charged at the white aliens and snatched their wands. She beat them with the wands, beat anything that came in her way.

The white aliens lost the battle. They got onto smaller vehicles and flew away.

From the stolen spaceship, the prisoners dragged out the dead bodies of other prisoners under order of the Imperials, who then cast aside the bodies and ordered the interior of the ship to be cleaned before marching the prisoners into the patrol ship as the day before. The bodies were stacked outside like so much trash. When they got to the patrol ship, they were again prodded with guns into groups of men and women and thrown into separate rooms.

The prisoners were given a rare, delicious feast that night. But very few of them ate without guilt or dread. Most of them were thinking of their fallen friends. As well as the Imperials who had forbidden them from using guns and shot them instead.

An announcement blared.

—Tomorrow, we attack the enemy's main base.

Isfobeddin entered the room and repeated the announcement. "We're attacking their base tomorrow."

The women didn't answer. A few shot her hostile looks. When Isfobeddin held out some extra food, someone slapped the tray out of her hands. It fell to the floor with a loud clang. Silence fell.

"Get out."

It was said by one of the women in a low but clear voice.

Isfobeddin, like always, smiled her cat smile. She left the cell.

*

Near dawn, she was shaken awake. In the dark, she could just make out Isfobeddin's features.

"What … what is—"

Her mouth was blocked by Isfobeddin's hand.

"Quiet. Don't make a sound. Just listen," Isfobeddin whispered, obviously tense. She had never seen her this anxious. "Make a run for it. Forget this war."

"What?"

Against her confusion, Isfobeddin rapidly whispered, "We're all dead. You, me, everyone here, we're already dead."

"What do you mean by that?"

"There's no place left for us to return to. So run. They will never give you your freedom."

Isfobeddin swiftly turned and made her way out of the cell.

The next day, the prisoners did not march.

Isfobeddin disappeared. Announcements kept issuing from the speakers, ordering everyone to find her. The prisoners were used not to attack the white aliens' base but to look for Isfobeddin in both the patrol ship and the captured white spaceship. As the search went on, the prisoners were called in one by one to be interrogated about what they knew of Isfobeddin.

She was also called to a narrow room and surrounded by gray uniforms. Naturally, she did not tell them about Isfobeddin's visit from the night before. Her Imperial wasn't fluent, and she made an effort to make it even more awkward than usual, irritating the guards until they kicked her out to rejoin the search for their fugitive.

Isfobeddin was found four days later. The Imperials brought all the prisoners into one place for her execution. Isfobeddin's face was swollen, her body was covered in blood, her hair was a mess, and she kept bleeding from the back of her left ear, which continuously trickled down her neck onto her torn dress.

"It's a lie! All of it! We were lied to!" she kept screaming from where she was tied.

The gray uniforms raised their guns at her.

"Malenka! Levinok!" Isfobeddin screamed. "My children! My babies!"

The gray uniforms fired.

Isfobeddin died.

The next day, the Imperials brought all of the prisoners out in front of the white spaceship. With the exception of a few gray uniforms, the Imperials got onto the patrol ship and left before them. The prisoners were made to follow on foot.

She plodded on. Her right wrist, injured during the fight for the white spaceship, was in incredible pain. Massaging it with her left hand, she ruminated over Isfobeddin's last moments, her screams, the names of her children, how it was "all" a "lie," how she should "make a run for it," and what it all meant.

Someone tapped her on the back. She turned.

"Excuse me."

It was a man. *The* man. The older man who had fallen beside her in the previous battle, who had a bullet go through his neck and spurted blood everywhere.

He looked very unsettled.

"Where exactly are we? And when did we land?"

She couldn't answer him.

Double Helix II

The dream of immortality was as old as myth in their history.

A long time ago, when humans knew nothing of science or technology and lived from day to day relying on the whims of nature, there was one king who dreamed of living a life that went beyond the existential conditions of his mortal being. The king sent his courtiers to many different lands and oceans on their planet, tasking them to find the elixir of immortality. The courtiers would bring from all over the world whatever medicines were said to hold the secret of forever life, which the king would then give to the old people of his land to try. If the potion made them sick, the king would put both courtier and old one to death, and if the old one died from the potion, the king would behead for treason not only the courtier who brought the potion but every member of his family.

The old ones brought forth before the king continued to die, the king continued to execute his courtiers and their families, and the courtiers who were left scattered to find the true elixir, but in secret they ran away from the kingdom. No one cared for the country's rivers and mountains. The people starved, and the air was always full of voices lamenting the executed and the exiled.

And so it came to pass that the people sent up a prayer and brought forth a witch. The witch waited until the day the king found the first white hairs of his temples and was lost in despair before paying him a visit. She made his servants leave the room and whispered to the king that she had brought him the elixir of immortality. As the king became suspicious and was about to call an old one like before, the witch stopped him.

—You are the immortal king, and therefore, the elixir will only take with you. If one who does not have the blood of kings takes the elixir, they will die immediately, and their body will become scattering ash.

The king could barely believe her. He stared into the deathly dark of the witch's eyes as she brought forth a pouch containing the elixir of immortality. Entranced by her gaze, the king found his hand slowly reaching for the elixir as the witch spoke again.

—There is a condition. As immortality is not permitted in men, you must pay the price for becoming more than man.

The king was suddenly anxious.

—What is that price? We are the king. We can give you all the gold and silver and glory your heart desires.

The witch shook her head.

—I shall have your memory.

This answer so unexpected that the king's hand paused in mid-air. The witch grinned, revealing her sharp teeth.

—You shall live as you have until now. You shall speak and walk and dance and tell one thing from another. But as you shall be more than man, I shall have your memories of your time when you were among men.

The king thought for a moment and then nodded. The witch

held out the pouch with the elixir. He took it from her and opened it. Inside it was not a liquid but two large silver pills.

The witch grinned once more.

—Enjoy your immortality forever.

She vanished.

The next day, the servants found the king in the gardens of the palace. He held a pouch in his hand and stood staring at the sky. He seemed healthy enough and answered questions, but he didn't seem to know who he was or what was his country. Even as he was led by the servants inside, he never let go of the pouch.

The king became a different person that day. No longer did he seek the elixir of life or kill his courtiers or old ones. When he was beseeched to take care of affairs of state, he did so in silence. The people were reassured, and the returning courtiers were pleased.

But the king seemed to remember nothing. Every morning, he would forget everything that had happened up to the day before. The king was ever more polite to the queen, but at the same time, he kept her at a distance and treated the crown prince like he was someone else's son.

The years passed and the prince grew up, and the queen and his courtiers and servants aged. The king did not change. Ever since the night he stared up at the stars as he held the pouch given to him by the witch, neither his body nor his soul changed even a little. Even when the queen passed away and the crown prince married and had his own prince, the king did not age at all beyond that day he first found a white hair on his temple. And then, when the king's grandson and granddaughter came of age, he finally spoke to the crown prince.

—We were a fool and made a foolish error. We shall bequeath you the kingdom now, in the hopes that you will not repeat such foolishness in your life.

—But what is this error of which you speak, Father?

The king had an answer.

—So preoccupied were we of escaping death that we knew not of what life truly is.

The king soon disappeared somewhere. It was said that no one saw or heard from him ever again.

When the king was gone, the crown prince opened the small pouch that he had left behind. Inside it were some silver crumbs of strange texture and smell that disintegrated in the breeze, and then all that was left was the empty pouch.

And so went the legend. That the king, having partaken of the witch's curse, still roams our world, not knowing what life is for he has never known death, and not knowing who himself is for he has no memory. Such a king is still among us.

4. *Birds*

She didn't know how to explain to someone who could not remember he had died that he had died.

The man remembered nothing. Not how they were taken prisoner by the white aliens, not saving her from drowning in the river, not killing a white alien by shooting through a tiny hole in their helmet. He remembered none of these when she mentioned them. There were no bullet wounds on his neck, entrance nor exit. Nor were there any wounds or scars on the man's hands and arms. There wasn't a trace of the struggle for survival he had been engaged in since being dumped on the surface of this planet by the Imperials.

"You're saying I'm dead," murmured the man. "That I was shot . . . ?"

He rubbed the back of his neck, lost in thought.

Because he didn't ask her anymore, she was a little reassured. The prisoners marched. The man marched beside her, still rubbing his neck. Neither she nor the man knew where they were going. All they could do was follow in the shadow thrown by the patrol vehicle that flew above them. As she marched with the man who did not remember his death, she thought of the young man who had also appeared before her more than once after he had been killed. She thought of the white aliens who were shot by him, who then slowly got up in the fog. Was there no death on this planet? Then where was it that death existed, and where did the dead go before they were brought back? Questions and more questions. No one would answer them, condemned as they were to echo without end in her mind.

Through the humming of the flying patrol vehicle and the sound of the prisoners talking and the Imperials who were on foot to herd them shouting, she thought she heard a piercing scream. Once, then twice. She tried to listen for them more carefully, but there was too much ambient noise to tell whether the sound was imagined or real.

"Do you hear that?" the man suddenly asked. "What's that sound?"

She looked at him. There it was again, the piercing scream. It was a bit closer this time. In a flash, she remembered where she had last heard that sound.

"Birds. Birds come," she said urgently. "Run! Run now!"

They were surrounded by rifle-wielding gray uniforms, and the patrol ship hovered above them, and beyond was the white wasteland. This planet didn't seem to have a single sheltering tree or rock or cave, just stretches of fine sand. As she desperately looked around them, she realized the birds were the only wild animals they had encountered since their landing, and aside from the white disk of the white aliens' spaceship, there wasn't a city, village, or even a house in sight. The whole planet was lifeless, white, and smooth.

Red Sword

And from that white and smooth horizon rose a black bird. No, not just one—a flock that soon covered the sky with their wingspans. The wind from their wings made the ground vibrate, and their cries seemed to shatter the atmosphere.

The prisoners screamed and scattered despite the Imperials making threats, but before the latter could even raise their rifles to shoot, they were set upon by the black birds and their claws and beaks, collapsing into blood-spurting piles of gray.

A sharp pain like a spear plunging through her ribs made her lose her balance. In the next moment, she was flying through the air.

She came to when she was tossed onto something cushiony. Her surroundings reeked. When she tried to sit up, pain from both sides of her ribcage convulsed her.

"What is, where are—ah!"

The man's voice made her look behind her.

They were riding on the wing of a giant black bird. The cushion she had felt was the feathers. They were not the feathers she was familiar with, but a kind of black fur covered with a thin membrane.

The man had screamed when he had tried to lean his hand on the middle of the wing and his hand had slid right off.

Through that black fur they heard a weak, inquisitive chirp. Little, furry white heads popped out from the black fur. The heads stared at her. As one of them approached, she found it cute and held out a hand.

Someone behind her grabbed her hand and pulled it back.

"Don't do that," the someone whispered. "They'll rip your fingers off."

She turned to see who had spoken to her.

Her own, pale face stared back at her.

She was speechless for a moment, gazing at this identical face.

"Who are you?" the other her said. "What's going on?"

She wanted to ask the same question. But before she could answer, she noticed two corpses next to the woman. Their faces had swollen so much they were beyond recognizable, but one corpse wore a deep indigo skirt and the other the remnants of some light green material.

"Tumina. Atung."

"You know those two?" whispered the woman who looked like her. "They were caught with me. The Imperials let us out by the river. We had crossed it and were drinking from it when the black birds came and snatched us up—" She coughed. Blood sprayed from her mouth and nose. She pressed her hand to them. She noticed that the woman who looked like her only had three fingers on her right hand. The hand was yellow and darkening and oozing with something.

Her coughs continued for a long time. When they seemed to stop, she began to have seizures.

Reflexively, she embraced the woman who looked like her, turned her face to the side so she would not swallow her own tongue, and held on until the seizures stopped.

Despite her seizure, she still tried to talk.

"But why … and how …"

She hugged her tighter and tried to calm her.

"It's all right. We'll talk later. Right now, we have to survive this place."

Red Sword

Even after the woman who looked like her stopped coughing blood and her seizures ceased, she kept holding her and stroking her back and placating her.

"We'll survive, we'll survive this together."

Silently, the man watched them nearby.

The black birds formed a flock and circled the air, their chicks on their backs. Their wingspans were vast, which meant the birds that flew circles at the edge of the flock created a draft that kept the birds carrying chicks in the middle of the flock suspended without movement. The women and the man were together on one of the middle birds. The white, fluffy chicks kept approaching them. When this happened, the woman who looked like her would brandish her scabbard—which looked just like hers—until they retreated, and she would collapse into coughs again. Her wound kept bleeding. Every movement seemed to subject the woman who looked like her to mortal pain. She had thought the chicks couldn't be that dangerous and that it wasn't worth her counterpart to expend so much energy on keeping them away. But when she saw how relentlessly they pecked at the remains of Indigo Skirt and Light Green Skirt, she changed her mind.

"Take my … sword." The woman who looked like her listlessly handed her a red scabbard and sword. "Ride … the birds …" In between her coughs, she added, "Not too harshly … the mother bird gets angry … gently … keep distance …" Her coughing overtook her.

She held the woman who looked like her to her chest and gripped the proffered scabbard.

Being up on the wing of the black bird was dizzying. The winds kept blowing, and the stench made her insides turn. The fur caused her skin to itch, making little red bumps stand up all over her hands. The white chicks kept trying to peck at them, and she had to keep holding the woman who looked like her to her chest while stealthily fending them off, trying not to attract the attention of the mother bird. It was exhausting work. She was tired and wanted to throw up from the smell and was very thirsty.

"Give me the sword," the man said, holding out his hand.

She shook her head. She could never give him the sword. It wasn't a question of trusting or not trusting the man. She couldn't give him her sword in the same way she couldn't give him her arm.

Instead, she unholstered the gun strapped to her thigh and handed it to him. He was taken aback.

"Where did you get this?"

The white chicks were attacking so she couldn't answer. The man examined the magazine.

"Just two bullets," he murmured in disappointment.

"Use well."

She waved away a particularly frisky chick, trying not to breathe in too much of the odor.

"You're very short with words," the man remarked.

"Imperial, don't know." She added, cuttingly, "*You* learn, my tongue."

The man shook his head and said no more on the matter.

She must've dozed off. Not a deep sleep but more of a passing out from the fatigue and stench.

"Bird!"

The man's shout startled her into consciousness. The white chicks were right in front of them with their beaks wide open. She struck out with her red scabbard, striking three of them in the head.

The chicks screamed.

Almost at the same time, one of the circling black birds turned its head their way. Its blood-red eyes stared right at her and descended to where she was, fanning great puffs of putrid air. A red claw swung for her. She ducked, the claw grasping air. A sound like tearing steel split her ear.

The wing they rode began to tilt. The bird they were on was trying to fight the attacking bird, their steel-like beaks crashing and a great wind being created around them. The two women and the man grabbed onto the black fur as best they could as they were tossed about.

The bodies of Indigo Skirt and Light Green Skirt fell from the bird and smashed into pieces in the melee on the way down, disappearing into the white of the ground.

The attacking black bird pecked at where Indigo Skirt had lain. The injured bird screeched and fought back. They lost their grip on the bird—the woman who looked like her held on to the wing bone with her uninjured hand, the woman grabbed her waist, and the man held onto the woman's ankles.

One of the white chicks gave a thin yelp as it was tossed overboard. The attacking black bird swooped off to save it. The other bird righted itself, and the women and the man found their balance again.

The fight was over. No more birds attacked. But the circling of the birds in the periphery had sped up, the mood tense.

The woman who looked like her leaned on her shoulder and coughed, rubbing the wrist on her uninjured side. Seeing this, she rubbed her injured counterpart's wrist instead.

As she did so, she thought of the bodies of Indigo Skirt and Light Green Skirt that had fallen to the ground. She had seen Tumina and Atung in the march before they'd been taken by the birds. Those bodies—they couldn't have been the real Indigo Skirt and Light Green Skirt. The real ones must still be alive somewhere.

But who were the real ones, in the end?

To her, the ones she knew were the real ones.

She thought of the vast white earth beneath them. She thought of what it would be like to fall from this bird and crash down there on that white expanse.

In war, the ones who survive are real. The surviving ones are the real ones.

She got herself together.

The birds began to descend. The women and the man tried their best not to slip from the wing and fall to the ground.

"They're going down to rest," the woman who looked like her shouted. "When we land by the river, water …"

She couldn't hear what came next. She nodded.

The black birds shrugged them off by the river. She and the man supported the woman who looked like her to the edge of the water. After she helped her injured twin drink and drank some for herself, she looked about her.

This was not the embankment where the white disk they stole from the white aliens was. They were surrounded by sharply pointed hills and cliffs, and like everywhere else on this planet, there wasn't a single tree in sight.

The black birds were digging a large pit in the white sands near one of the cliffs. Each bird took their chick from the nursery bird to bed down in the pit.

"That's where we spend the night with them," whispered the woman who looked like her.

"When they fall asleep, let's run," she whispered.

The birds did not fall asleep. If either woman or the man so much as stirred, a white chick would rear its head and its mother would wake to stare down at them. The woman who looked like her kept coughing and whimpering—she tried not to, but she couldn't help vomiting blood and gritting her teeth and shuddering and crying. To not attract the attention of the birds, the uninjured woman kept holding her and stroking her. She thought of stories to distract the woman who looked like her.

"Remember the story about the flute?" she whispered in the ear of her twin. "It was your favorite as a child."

The woman who looked like her, her head resting on her chest, nodded very slightly. "A long, long time ago …" she whispered before beginning to cough again, so her carer held her and rocked her and whispered the story to her instead.

A long, long time ago, there lived a young woman in a village surrounded by mountains and an ocean. The young woman was diligent, waking up at dawn to gather clams from the sea and catch fish or going to the mountains for herbs and kindling. One dawn, at the beach, she saw something very strange floating on the water. It looked like a fish carrying a large conch. When a wave hit them, the two would separate, and when it had passed, they would reunite. Whenever they reunited, the conch on the back of the fish would shine with the light of the coming dawn. It was such a beautiful sight that while the conch was on the fish's back, the young woman caught the fish, separated the conch, and made a flute out of it …

"… and when the young woman played the conch flute, amazing things happened …" whispered the woman who looked like her with a smile.

Her sister continued, "The storms would calm when she played the flute …"

"And in droughts it would rain when she played the flute …"

"And in the spring the butterflies would come, and in the summer the birds would sing in time with her when she played the flute …"

"And in the evenings and mornings," the woman who looked like her whispered weakly, "the animals would come out of the forest to listen to her play …"

"Do you remember how she helped the bear caught in the snare with her flute?" She stroked the hair of the woman who looked like her.

The other woman nodded in answer. "Of course … She befriends the bear and they go off in search of treasure together …"

"You liked that treasure the best, right?"

They both looked at each other then. Wide, silent smiles.

Red Sword

"You were so looking forward to learning what the treasure was, right?"

"In the end, it was a cat. Good at catching rats and fish, a clever and wise cat." Some color returned to the cheeks of the woman who looked like her.

"And," she said, grasping the other woman's left hand, the uninjured one, "the cat was good at catching birds."

"Do you think we can ever get back home?"

"Of course we can." She nodded vigorously. "You and me, we are going to survive and go back home."

Another smile spread on the pale face of the woman who looked like her. She suddenly started coughing into her hands, as quietly as possible. The effort of suppressing it made even the woman who was holding her tight shake as well.

When the coughs subsided, the man lightly tapped her shoulder. Wordlessly, he gestured with a cock of the head.

She looked to where he was indicating.

The birds were not moving.

She looked back at the man. The man closed his eyes and brought his hands together and laid his head on them, miming sleep. She nodded.

"Let's go," she whispered, grasping the hand of the woman who looked like her. She received a determined nod in answer.

The man led the way. She carried the woman who looked like her on her back. They began to crawl up the white sandy pit.

The white sand was fine, and the slightest weight made it crumble. The man concentrated on ensuring each hand and foothold was secure before putting his weight on it.

This made their climb very slow. She almost lost her footing many times when the woman on her back began to convulse.

"I'm sorry," the other woman whispered through bloody foam and coughs.

Whenever she said that, she would reply, "We are going to survive this together."

The woman who looked like her continued to stifle her coughs into her back, and she slowly followed the man up the footholds, repeating again and again, "You and me, we're going to survive and go back home."

It was what she herself wanted to hear.

The man made it out of the pit. She was far behind him.

"Quickly!" he whispered, holding out his hand to her.

A sharp scream made him fall backwards in surprise.

From behind her and the woman on her back, who held tightly onto a red scabbard in her uninjured hand, a black bird with eyes as red as blood and an enormous beak was rising.

The man fired. One bullet bounced off the black bird's hard beak, having no impact. The other hit the bird directly in the bright crimson eye.

Her eardrums almost tore from the ensuing screech. Blood from the bird's wound splattered everywhere. The woman on her back was hit with some of the splatter, which made her scream in pain.

She climbed as quickly as she could. The bird, in the throes of pain, was slamming its beak against the walls of the pit, making the white sand crumble. She tried to carry the weight on her back and stay out of the way of the frightening black beak as she attempted to run vertically up the walls of the pit before it collapsed.

The scabbard suddenly crossed her throat. The woman on her back screamed once more. She must be caught by the bird, by claw or by beak.

So she even more desperately tried to make her way up the walls. The scabbard around her neck made breathing impossible. But she couldn't tell the other woman to let go. They had to survive and go back home together. Together . . .

The man's hand appeared from nowhere and grabbed her. He pulled, and she grabbed her twin's hand that was choking her with the scabbard, and the man managed to bring them both over the lip of the pit.

"Can you run?" she shouted as she lowered the woman who looked like her from her back upon the white sands. She was out of breath.

But the other woman didn't answer. The eyes on her pale face were unfocused. From the back of her head down her neck and back were giant peck marks from the bird. Through her tattered flesh, parts of her skull and vertebrae and ribs were visible.

*

"We must run." The man grabbed her arm and raised her to her feet. "Run!"

Almost at the same time, the bird screeched again, bringing her to her senses. She picked up the red scabbard that her twin hadn't let go of even in death.

With the man, she began to run.

They ran. They dove into the river. The clear water side was dark and threatening, and the white water side was dim and heavy and suffocating. After crossing the water, she followed the man as they continued to run downstream.

After a long while, she collapsed, completely out of breath. "Wait, wait." She called for the man to stop. "No, sound."

"What?" The man looked behind at her. "What are—"

"Bird."

The man stopped. He came back to her.

There was calm all around. The birds had not pursued them across the river. They seemed to have returned to the white, sandy pit where their chicks were.

The man waited for her to catch her breath. Once she had, the two slowly walked downriver in search of their people. As they walked, she wept.

She hadn't shed tears when the young man died, or when the older man died. Not even when she became a prisoner of the white aliens, or when the leader of the white aliens sentenced her to death, or when the two of them, their hands tied, awaited their execution atop the embankment by the white disk. Now she cried as she walked, grasping to her chest a sword and scabbard, identical to hers, once owned by a woman, identical to her.

The man said nothing. He accompanied her in silence on this unfamiliar planet as she tearfully mourned the loss of her twin, with no remains to show for it, only her red sword in her embrace.

Double Helix III

The first black birds obediently came back. The researchers hatched more black birds and implanted a greater variety of memories. These birds flew off to more parts of the white planet. Some birds returned immediately, others returned later, and still others never returned.

As the researchers continued to release and receive the birds, they began making not artificial eggs but artificial wombs to grow humans in. The manufactured humans were given the memories of the black birds and the name of a mythical human king from long ago. Depending on the purpose of the experiment, some were implanted with memories of the past and others with past languages. And they observed whether these manufactured human beings advanced from their pasts and evolved toward the researchers' present, and if the latter were possible, how close the manufactured beings could come to their makers.

The ultimate test was supposed to be to send these human beings to the white planet to see if they could survive. Conditions on the white planet were harsh, and aside from the white river with the opaque water and the black birds they had also created, there wasn't much life in sight. If the manufactured human beings could survive, it would prove that they could possess another colony there. And in that colony would be the endless potential of the white earth and dim sky and their manufactured humans and animals. So enamored were they of this possibility that they overlooked the fact that it was not so easy to rule over sentient beings.

The women born of the artificial wombs all started menstruating on the same day. And on that very day, every black bird came back.

The researchers were standing outside the spaceship to greet the birds. The birds attacked. They pecked with their beaks and tore with their claws. The researchers fled back into the spaceship.

Just when they were taking out their weapons and arming them to kill the birds, the captain, who was also the head researcher, stopped them. The black birds were, after all, results of their experiments and therefore valuable property. Without the permission of the Empire, they could never damage the birds, declared the captain and head researcher.

The black birds were lifeforms that they had made. Surely they could come up with a safe way to control them. The head researcher armed himself with a snare and taser that he had used when bringing up the birds and went outside the spaceship.

Those inside the spaceship witnessed their head researcher being picked up in the beak of one of the birds and being snapped in half, bone fragments and exposed organs falling from the white sky, staining the ground below red with his blood. Even after there was no one to attack, the black birds didn't leave. They tried to smash the spaceship, pecking and clawing at the hatch in particular.

The captain was dead, but this didn't change the fact that the black birds were the result of an experiment and the property of the Empire. So they called the Empire, reporting their status, begging for reinforcements, help, a solution, advice, or an order to leave. They knew, of course, that any response to such a message would take at least twenty years of their home planet time to receive. In the various expeditionary forces of the Empire, there were actual explorers and also researchers disguised as explorers. The existence of the latter was confidential, and the forces did not know each other's locations or what situation they were in. There was no hope of receiving help, but nevertheless they requested assistance and a plan of action to move forward.

The birds, day and night, would scratch and peck and claw at the spaceship, but one day, as suddenly as they'd come, they flew away. The researchers held their breath and waited. The birds did not come back.

They immediately stopped growing new birds. The artificial eggs they had remaining, they froze along with the newly hatched chicks. They needed more humans. The more the better. To protect them and to protect the research results and establish a colony on the white planet and open for them a new world and new possibilities.

It was the first women who set out to find the black birds. The first menstruating women were the first to enter the battlefield. The birds loved blood, and the women would bleed persistently for days. The birds could smell it, it drew them in from vast distances. The researchers had managed to figure out that much from their previous observations of the birds.

Just as the black birds were a result of experiments and research, so too were the humans born from artificial wombs. The researchers couldn't discard the results of their experiments without authorization from the Empire. And after all, their research results battling each other could in itself be an experiment. They decided to choose the easiest and least risky way to solve their problem.

When memories of the birds were implanted into the women's minds, the women began attacking the researchers. The researchers threatened the women and punished them. The women did not comply.

The researchers then showed the women the other women being developed in the artificial wombs. They appealed to the women saying that if they found and got rid of the black birds and told them how they did it in the process, they would release these new women.

The women agreed to it. And so, with no weapons and with their bleeding bodies, they set out.

The women did not return.

5. *Stars in the Emptiness*

In the emptiness above, there were stars that ate the air.

Her silent questions about what this war truly was and who she truly was, questions she couldn't answer, suddenly stopped. The stars in the emptiness were round and translucent and iridescent and floated in a flock as they ate the fog. Neither of them knew what they were, and they stared at this novel scene, awe-struck. The floating half-spheres, for that was what they were, that sparkled and shone with variegated lighting, were eating the fog and leaving a clear space where the flock had passed through. The flying objects were beautiful in a way she had never known before.

As if bewitched, she began to walk toward them. The man grabbed her arm.

"We don't know what it is," he whispered. "No matter how beautiful they are, they could be monsters like those black birds."

While she thought the half-spheres were too beautiful to be monsters, she stood back. As they watched, the air-eating half-sphere flock that sparkled and shone in different colors circled the riverbank before floating above the river, cutting through the fog before eating it.

And in the spaces where they had eaten away the fog, they saw white aliens across the river. There were two of them, and they stood on the riverbank staring intently into the river, engaged in some mysterious task.

They looked about them. Like everywhere else on this white planet, there were no trees, rocks, houses, or anything on the embankment. There was no place for them to hide.

And the white aliens saw them. The two humans froze.

Would they shoot at them from the other side or cross the river to kill them? The white aliens did not move. They stared at her and the man and took turns pressing the thighs of their protective suits. The vibrations that resulted from the soles of their feet were their method of communication, she knew well enough by now. The white aliens were discussing something.

"What could they be discussing," she wondered aloud in her language.

"Calling big boat or watching boat?" the man said next to her.

He hadn't spoken in Imperial. It had been his native tongue. But oddly enough, she could understand him. The words were strange and sounded exotic to her ear, but he had obviously said something like, "Maybe they are calling the mothership or the patrol ship?"

"River, swim, escape?" she said in her stilted Imperial.

The man shook his head. "We can't breathe under there, how long can you stay under?"

"Where, then?"

Before he could answer, a gigantic white alien sprang from the river.

The man brandished his gun as he stepped in front of her. But she remembered, suddenly, that he had used up his two bullets. Before she could warn him, before she could even open her mouth, the giant white alien picked up the man and threw him. Like a rock or a broken branch, the man lifted easily and arced through the air before falling into the river.

The giant turned to her. She unsheathed her sword. As the giant approached, she looked closely at the space between their face and neck.

But there was no gap there.

This wasn't a white alien wearing power armor. It was a machine.

The machine raised its fearful arms toward her.

She ran. She returned her sword to its sheath and ran.

There was no point in fighting a machine. The sword left to her by the woman who looked like her did not have a broken-off tip or a chipped blade, but it was woefully inadequate to use against the hulk of metal before her. Just one swipe of a machine arm and her sad little sword would snap in two. If the white aliens fired their rays, she could use the mirrors on her scabbard to reflect them back, but there was nothing to be done about a machine. All it did was charge at you with its incredibly strong arms. Which was why she was intent, now, on escaping their grasp.

She fell. The sand of the riverbank was white and soft and her feet sank in it every time she took a step, making running difficult. The machine slammed its fist down toward her face—she rolled away just in time.

The sand was so soft and the machine so strong that its fist was buried deep in the sand, and it struggled to extract itself. Slinging her scabbard on her shoulder, she started to climb up its sunken arm.

The arm had many seams that were easy to use as handholds. But when she grabbed ahold of one seam, it snapped open and black liquid poured out. Surprised, she grabbed another seam. It also snapped open, but there was nothing inside. She hung from it and got her foot onto it and climbed higher.

The machine had paused as it watched her climb its arm, but when she had opened the seam that made the black liquid spurt, it tried to slap at her with its free arm like she was a bug. She kept ducking to the other side of the arm, avoiding its strikes, and the machine ended up damaging its own arm. She grabbed ahold of a seam near its armpit and swung herself up to its shoulder. The arm tried to come for her again. She leaped behind its neck.

Flailing, the machine attempted to catch her with its damaged and undamaged arms. Its back was full of neat, smooth metal bumps, and she held on at the nape of the machine's neck as she avoided the blows coming from both sides. There were no handholds below that point, and if she slipped from where she was, she would fall and be instantly crushed to death.

Desperately holding on, she tried to look for what might be a weak spot. Between the neck and head, the shoulder and arm … All that met the eye were smooth seams, nothing that was particularly wide or narrow or protruding.

But there—a seam on the shoulder. Next to it was a small depression in the metal that seemed to invite being pressed. She accepted the invitation.

The entire back of the machine opened. A black substance with a terrible stench burst out of the machine. She was knocked off her handhold and slid down the machine. As terrible as the smell of the black substance was, it broke her fall. She coughed and gagged, getting up and shaking the substance off her. Her whole body began to itch. The stench and itching and rising red bumps on her skin made her think of when she was riding the black bird. She thought of the woman who looked like her. Her shredded flesh, her exposed ribs, her pupils that had lost their focus.

Its back lid open wide, the machine turned to look at her. Was it trying to decide whether to gather up the black substance and shove it back in itself or kill her?

Before it could make a decision, she ran. She ran right between its legs. The machine tried to turn and grab her at the same time—it lost its balance and fell.

She dove into the river.

Across the river, the man was fighting the two white aliens.

He had briefly lost consciousness when he hit the water. As he sank into the white depths, the pressure on his lungs made him come to his senses, and he swam, not knowing which direction was up but swimming anyway, desperate for air. The fact that he managed to find his way into the clear part and back up to the other side of the river was a miracle. And the first thing he saw as he caught his breath and looked up was the firing end of a white wand.

Reflexively, he raised his arms and was about to get up when the boot of the white alien caught his eye, and he grabbed it and pulled. The white alien fell backward, his wand firing over the man's head.

The white alien next to him fired. The ray seared the flesh of his back as it grazed him. The man fell, screaming.

The fallen white alien grabbed the wand they had dropped when they fell, and the man leaped to seize hold of their wrist. He fired at the other white alien with it, and held on tight to the wrist before finding an opportunity to twist it and fire at the helmet. Several times.

She dragged herself out of the river. As soon as she did so, she looked back at the bank across from her.

The machine was still unmoving. The white fog and tepid air made it difficult to see too clearly—she kept peering into the obscurity. When she was satisfied the dark hunk across the water was truly not moving, she turned her gaze to the man.

He was still striking down at the white alien with the wand. The white alien wasn't moving, and the smashed part of their helmet the man kept hitting was turning red and light pink.

Using all her strength, she got herself to her feet. She slowly approached the man. Not having the strength to speak, she gently placed a hand on his shoulder.

Startled, he whipped around and stared at her.

"Dead," she said, pointing at the white alien.

The man, struggling a little, stood up. His face had turned pale, and his eyes were unfocused. She supported him on one side to lead him away to the white sands, where she sat him down. The man's right fist had translucent fragments of helmet stuck into it as well as white blood mixing with his red.

She slowly spread his hand. He made a grimace as she pried the wand out of his grasp. Then, she pincered out the helmet fragments one by one. He grimaced again but let her do it.

Once she had taken out all the fragments she could see, she went to the river, took up some water in her hands, and came back to the man to wash his hands with it. She did this a few more times until both the red and white blood were washed away, and she looked carefully to see if she had missed any other lodged fragments. When she was satisfied his hands were clean, she unsheathed her sword.

"Clothes, cut. May I?"

The man's eyes were still unfocused, and it wasn't apparent he was listening, but he nodded.

Using the tip of her sword, she carefully cut off one of the man's sleeves and tore it into strips. She soaked one of the strips and wiped the man's hands with it. Checking one more time for fragments, she then wrapped the hand with one of the dry strips as a bandage.

"Stand, can?"

He didn't answer. He was looking at her though, so she repeated her question.

"Stand, can?"

His eyes, as she stared back at him, slowly regained their focus. She helped him stand up.

"Walk," she whispered. "Can?"

The man nodded. This time, he clearly understood the situation. This reassured her.

Just as they were about to continue their walk down the river, the white alien without the smashed helmet started to stir.

In surprise, they stopped in their tracks. The white alien slowly raised their upper body, leaning on their right hand. There was a small hole in their chest plate, and white liquid was running from it in a thin stream.

The white alien pressed their leg using their left hand. The white sands vibrated.

"Don't know." The woman shook her head. "Your language, don't know."

The white aliens made the sand vibrate again. Even more disconcerted, she shook her head once more. Grasping at their wound, the white alien tried to get to their feet.

The translucent star cluster hovering over the milky side of the river suddenly zoomed toward the white alien, the multicolored lights eating through the fog as they landed on the white alien's chest.

The formation of stars slowly turned white. As they whitened, they expanded. The white alien underneath the stars began to spasm, thrashing the sand desperately with their limbs and vibrations.

The vibrations intensified, as did the spasms, and the demi-sphere stars turned an opaque white. The white alien's spasms stopped. As did the vibrations in the sand.

As the demi-sphere stars sucked the blood of the white alien, she started to slowly move back with the man. They were ready to run at any moment, but they could not take their horrified and fascinated eyes off what was happening before them. When the white alien became still, the cluster of white stars, more voluminous than before, slowly and heavily floated back to the river, regained their multicolored flashing, and silently vanished into the fog.

They stared into the whiteness where the stars had gone.

When they were sure they wouldn't return, she went up to the remains of the white alien to take a closer look.

Their armor layer looked deflated somehow. Inside the translucent helmet visor, she could tell the white face had shrunken in to the skull as if the body had been sucked of all moisture.

"Gun," said the man. "We need their guns. Because ours doesn't have bullets."

She nodded. Carefully, she removed one of the gloves from the white alien's now-shriveled hands. It gave way easily. The revealed hand was parched to its fingertips.

Shaking, she handed the glove, the wand that the white alien had dropped by them, and the thicker wand holstered to their belt to the man. He looked puzzled as he held out his uninjured left hand to receive them, so she explained the wands didn't work unless they were held by the glove or were in contact with the armor.

"You, discovered," she added. "You, before death."

He looked troubled at this and averted his gaze.

The corpse of the other white alien in the bashed helmet did not give up its gloves as easily, not having been sucked dry by the multicolored star cluster. She tried a few times and gave up, went back to the man, took the glove and a wand from him, and fired a ray so it sliced the white alien's wrist. She shook out the severed hand from the glove and took the two wands from this body as well.

Flabbergasted, the man said, "Is that also something I discovered? Cutting the wrist?"

"I couldn't get the glove off so I had no choice. They're already dead, anyway." She said this in her own language, not in her awkward Imperial.

The man shook his head. He went to the water and drank from it and washed his face. She followed suit. They began walking once more.

As they walked, the man asked, "What kind of person was I? Before my death."

"Gun, shoot, well," she replied without thinking.

"Just that?"

She nodded. The man grinned, a little perplexed.

That was the only answer she could really give him. She didn't even know the man's name. The only thing she knew about his private life was that he had relations with Isfobeddin so that he could get his hands on some weapons. But Isfobeddin was dead, and there was no point in saying such things to the man.

Instead, she told him of the battles they had fought together and the time they'd been captured by the white aliens and freed by the other prisoners. And that his handling of his gun made her think she should learn how to shoot as well.

"Is that why you carry this around?" the man said as if reminded of something and handed her back the young man's gun. "I suppose a sword is better than a gun because it doesn't need bullets."

She nodded and accepted the gun proffered to her. There was no need to explain the gun's provenance to the man. Instead, she talked about the white aliens and their imperviousness to stabbing but not slicing, that the weakness in their armor was the point between the head and shoulders.

"But why are we at war?" he said. "I thought we would be given our freedom if we won, but the fact that there was another me … and that … that other person …" He gestured vaguely in the air.

She thought of the woman who looked like her, with her three remaining fingers on her festering right hand and her heartbreaking cough. She gritted her teeth, screwed her eyes shut, and shook her head.

"I don't know what is what anymore," said the man. "Who I am, what I'm doing here …"

She nodded. She thought of Isfobeddin's words. *Make a run for it. Forget this war. We're all dead. You, me, everyone here, we're already dead.*

She started to tell him about Isfobeddin.

They walked for a long time downriver until she couldn't walk anymore. She collapsed on the white sands.

"Are you tired?"

She nodded.

The man sat next to her. She looked up at the sky. It was, as always, dim and gray.

"I can never tell from that sky if it's night or day."

She nodded again. The man stopped talking then.

Her eyelids felt heavy, too heavy. Soon, she dozed off.

A scream. Frightened awake, she spent a moment in confusion, not knowing where she was.

Her eyes met the man's stare. He jumped to his feet, hiding his injured right hand behind him. She backed away slowly, her hands spread out before her in a *calm down* gesture. The man stared at her for a little more before finally coming to his proper senses.

"I'm sorry," he said.

"Water," she replied.

Obediently complying, he went to the river and drank some of the water. She went with him to drink and wash her face.

Then, without any further discussion, they began their walk again.

"Dream?" she asked as they walked.

The man nodded.

"What?" she asked again. The man shook his head and didn't answer. And she didn't ask anymore.

"Black birds tried to suck my blood," the man suddenly said as they walked. "You died … I mean, not you, but that woman who looked exactly like you …"

He trailed off and she nodded, not knowing what to say to that.

"And I … died …" he mumbled.

She switched sides to his left and gently held his uninjured hand. The man gave an answering squeeze.

They walked like this, hand in hand. She thought of the way he had struck down on the already dead white alien's helmet. The splatter of his blood, of the white blood all over the jagged edges of the shattered visor.

And she thought of the white spaceship. Of Isfobeddin and the gray uniforms shouting at them that it was a trophy of war and they were not allowed to shoot. Of the man who had bled to death next to her, shot through his neck.

The white aliens were said to be monsters that had invaded the Empire's territory. But she wondered if it wasn't the Imperials who had been the ones to steal the white aliens' planet.

Red Sword

That the Empire was making them complicit in their theft. In her broken Imperial, she rambled on about these thoughts for a bit to the man, who held her hand and listened and did not say anything.

She saw the banners of red and blue skirts. The man didn't remember these skirts tied to scabbards, and so she was the one to recognize them. She dropped his hand and ran toward the women, shouting gladly.

The women were now wearing the trousers of the men or the Imperials instead of the skirts that had kept winding around their legs. She quickly looked among the banners for the indigo and light green skirts and ran to them. She hugged them over and over again as they gazed back at her with dazed expressions.

"We were looking for you," Indigo Skirt said, "everyone thought you were dead, but we didn't want to believe it so we kept looking for you." Tears fell from her eyes.

She quickly told them of their dead counterparts on the wing of the black bird. That there was also someone who looked exactly like herself, that she had died while they were escaping the nest at night.

By the time she told them about the white aliens' machines and the black liquid, some gray uniforms approached. They grabbed her and started dragging her away. As she objected, they said, "You have deserted us during battle. We shall make an example of you by executing you before the other prisoners."

"Not! Escape! No!" she shouted. "White monster! Fight! Look!"

She showed them the glove and two wands of different

thicknesses she had taken from the white aliens.

The Imperials let go of her arm. They examined the weapons. One of the gray uniforms took the weapons away somewhere while the others stood guard around her.

The one that had gone away with her weapons came back and spoke in rapid Imperial to the others, too rapid for her to follow. They began dragging her away again. She screamed and struggled, but when she realized they weren't taking her to a clearing but to the patrol ship, she stopped struggling. Isfobeddin had been executed outside of the patrol ship and tossed aside. If they were going to kill her, they would not go through the bother of dragging her in and out of the patrol ship before doing it.

She turned out to be right. The Imperials pushed her into a dark cell instead. As she rolled on the floor, she was afraid the guards would beat or rape her. But after the gray uniforms threw her into the dark, they left her there and locked the door behind them.

The darkness was somehow reassuring to her. After making her way through the white fog not knowing when she would be attacked by the white aliens or by wild animals, it was actually comforting to be surrounded by narrow walls in the privacy of darkness. Breathing in the filtered air of the ship instead of the tepid, alien air of the planet was almost sweet. She did the best she could to stretch her legs in the small space and hugged her scabbard, once again marveling in gratitude at the fact that the Imperials never seemed to take their swords away from them, and the feeling warmed her so much that she soon let down her guard and fell asleep.

Her eyes opened of their own accord. The narrow cell was still dark. She could hear footsteps outside. Once again, she tensed up.

The narrow door partially opened. A tray containing water and food slid inside. The door shut again, leaving her alone in the dark once more.

She ran to the tray. Aside from the river water, she hadn't consumed anything in days. The small, rough bits of food on the tray was like a feast to her. She ate it up with gladness.

As she picked the food off the tray, her fingers touched something in the bottom of the food, round and hard things. She finished her food and picked up the hard things and rolled them about in her hand. They were cylindrical, with one end pointy and the other flat. Bullet-shaped.

They were bullets.

She counted them. A dozen.

She checked the gun that was strapped to her inner thigh. She didn't know how many bullets the young man's gun could be loaded with or even how to load the gun at all. But now she had a gun and twelve bullets to go with it.

She dragged the tray to her side and fondled the bullets in her hand. Her stomach was full, she was well-rested, and her mind was clearing by the minute.

A scream. Something smashed against the other side of her wall. More screams, in an incoherent language.

It was the man's voice.

She knocked on the wall, irritated at herself for not knowing or never once asking the man's name.

He screamed again and she slammed her palm against the wall. "Dream. Bad dream," she said. She gave another knock. "Wake."

The screaming stopped. She knocked again.

"Calm down. Water, food, eat."

"Who is that!" the man shouted. She thought of saying her name but changed her mind.

"Sword. Red sword."

The voice beyond the wall became silent. Alarmed, she knocked again.

"Are you also incarcerated?" said the man.

"Yes."

A long pause. "Are you going to stay there?"

She smiled a little. "Can't leave."

Silence again. She waited a moment longer and softly knocked.

"What is it?"

"Bullet, gun, load. Teach me."

The man, in a drowsy voice, slowly explained it to her. She followed his instructions, taking the magazine out and slipping in the bullets one by one.

In the midst of his explaining, the man's voice ceased. She assumed he had fallen asleep. Learning how to load just one bullet was enough, and she finished on her own with the remaining eleven. Then, working backwards from when she took it out, she fit the magazine back into the gun. Carefully, she strapped the loaded gun onto her inner thigh once more.

She then hugged her scabbard close again and laid back. In the narrow, safe darkness, she put her head against where the man's head would be on the other side of the wall and fell asleep. Both of them enjoyed a dreamless, deep, and satisfying sleep.

6. *Night on the Planet*

Night came to the planet. The gray uniforms flung open her cell door, dragged her out of the small and cozy darkness, and tossed her into the procession of exhausted prisoners outside. The air outside was as tepid and foggy as ever, but there was a red of sunset in it. The earth and sky were all red. She had thought this planet was in a perpetual dimly off-white day, but its sun, which she'd thought never set, was setting after all.

"Are you hurt?" Indigo Skirt worriedly asked as she helped her to her feet. Indigo Skirt still wore the gray trousers of the Imperials, her skirt torn in half with each strip tied to her scabbard at her belt.

Light Green Skirt watched her knock white dust off her knees and asked, angrily, "Did those bastards do anything to you?"

"They did nothing." She assured Light Green Skirt that she had only eaten some and slept. She didn't mention the bullets hiding in her tray. It was her turn to ask a question. "Why are you all wearing trousers?"

The women were all wearing the gray uniform trousers of the Imperials or the dark-colored ones of the men. She was the only one wearing her red skirt, torn as it was.

Light Green Skirt looked down at herself with a disgusted look and only shook her head. Indigo Skirt answered instead.

"After the black bird came and went, the Imperials suddenly gave them to us. Many soldiers must've died. They said there were too few people left for us to just sit around appreciating the view and we should go out there and be human shields."

"They didn't even give us weapons?" she murmured.

"Weapons?" sneered Light Green Skirt. "For human shields?"

But bullets weren't the only thing threatening the prisoners. She told them about the beautifully sparkling demi-sphere beings that sucked the white aliens dry of their moisture.

"You can't just go up to them because they're pretty. There are many dangerous things that live by the river."

And since they were talking, she also told them about the black, stinking substance that made her think of the black bird's wings, and how the machine had hoarded it in itself, and the fact that there were no domiciles of the white aliens of any sort that she'd seen.

"No barracks, no houses. There isn't a single tree or any real plants. No fish in the river, either. If we wanted food, we'd have to hunt down the black bird or those translucent blood-sucking things. Would that even be possible?"

Indigo Skirt and Light Green Skirt brooded over this.

"You said there were people who looked exactly like us, dead on the black bird's wing?" Light Green Skirt asked suddenly.

She nodded.

"Was it really us? Not just people who looked like us?"

"It was us. Face, clothes, scabbards, identical."

And memories. She remembered telling her favorite childhood fairy tale to the woman who looked like her as she lay in her embrace. She thought of her pale face and blackening right hand. She thought of how on this chaotic and incomprehensible and frightening planet, she had lost the one person whom she understood fully and who had fully understood her, a loss so painful there were no human words to describe it. Tears welled.

"Your man died and came back too," said Indigo Skirt thoughtfully.

"He's not my man," she replied indignantly, blinking away her tears. She told them about the man not remembering anything, that he knew only that the ship had landed on this planet and didn't remember anything that happened after, how he died or what kind of person he'd been.

"Can he be the same person but a different one?" said Indigo Skirt. "Can there be many people who look like us?"

"How can that be possible?" said Light Green Skirt. "What does that make us?"

The three women looked at one another, uncertainty in their eyes. No one knew how to answer that question.

The man was also released, dragged out into the open from deep sleep. In the white dust he blinked, trying to finish waking up, and stared up at the red sky. The white fog persisted in his brain. Slowly, he stood and caught up with the march, yawning.

"Must've been a fun night," someone said, elbowing his side.

The man, still sleepy, reflexively turned toward the other man who had touched him. It was a skinny and tall middle-aged man, someone he didn't know, leering at him.

"Finding it hard coming back to fight after a night with that tramp?"

The man tried to ignore the skinny man but was grabbed by the elbow before he could walk away.

"Rat! Traitor—"

He shook off the man's arm before he could finish his litany of insults. The skinny man continued to shout at him, glaring at him.

Other men gathered. Some tried to calm the skinny man down. Others took his side. Various voices and insults rang in the air. Gray uniforms came running, rifles raised. The man quickly dispersed with the rest of the crowd while the gray uniforms struck down the still-shouting skinny man with their rifle butts.

The man quickly made his way to the front of the march. From there, he plodded on through the red night.

The sky turned blood-red, then a crimson-tinged black. Formations of white aliens stood waiting for them. White spaceships filled the black horizon. The spaceships screamed in unison in an artificial voice.

—Sur-r-r-r-ender.

The prisoners stopped their march and stared at the countless white spaceships in the black sky.

—Sur-r-r-r-ender.

The patrol ship of the Empire began to land. The Imperials raised their rifles at the white spaceships.

Without a sound, the white spaceships in silent unison shot out white rays that split the black night sky and the earth beneath. The indifference and sheer silence of the attack belied their casually murderous intent. The emotionless efficiency of it filled the prisoners with a primal fear.

The Imperials and prisoners, and anyone standing outside the patrol ship, began to run. No one knew where they were running to. There wasn't a tree or a rock in sight. The only place anyone could hide was in the patrol ship, and once the Imperials made it inside, they slammed the airlock in the faces of the prisoners who had tried to follow them. The patrol ship's engines whirred up, and the prisoners who were desperate enough to cling to the ship screamed and fell away as the heat and smoke from the exhaust burned them.

As the patrol ship rose, a white spaceship soundlessly fired a white ray that directly hit its target mid-air, making the patrol ship crash onto the prisoners underneath. More white rays rained down from the red-black sky. Those who were running away were killed, as were those who couldn't run away. They were sliced in half by the white rays, crushed underneath the crashed patrol ship, hit by shrapnel and bled to death, or died otherwise in ways they knew not how or why.

The man ran. He ran to save his own life and to find her.

But the man could not make it to where the woman was. The white rays were raining down at random all around him, and he tried to run to the crashed patrol ship like all the other prisoners were doing. But the airlock was still shut. The ground beneath his feet was ringing from the destruction all around him, and as he ran away from the crash site in the chaos of white rays, he lost consciousness.

*

She hid herself in the remains of the crashed patrol ship. The second she saw the white spaceships rising in the red-black sky, a small voice that was her survival instinct had suggested in a whisper that she should run. Which was how she managed to run a little, just a little faster than the others in the opposite direction. When the patrol ship crashed, she had been too far to die from the shrapnel or be crushed. She had seen a large metal bulkhead, bent out of shape and planted firmly into the ground, and took refuge behind it. The white rays just barely missed the panel several times. A piece of it sliced off without a sound right next to her elbow. Readying herself to make a run for it, she stared ahead, waiting for a lull in the firing.

When she turned her head, she was surprised to see someone there with her. A plump man frightened to the point of looking pale, someone she didn't know very well, another prisoner.

"May I hide here with you?" he whispered in Imperial.

"Don't know," she whispered back. "Attack, here, slice, must run."

The pale-faced man she didn't know wasn't listening. He came closer to her and crouched right beside her. Half of his back was exposed because he was right under the sliced-off part, so she made herself smaller and gave him more room. The pale man leaned against the narrow bulkhead and sat right up against her. She stuck her head out and took her bearings of the unfolding situation outside.

Something damp touched her exposed arm. Surprised, she looked back.

The pale man she didn't know was stroking her arm with his sweaty hand.

She drew her arm away. "What?"

"You slept with that man, right?" the man whispered. She didn't understand. She stared back at him, confused.

"You were with him for several days? You had that black bird attack as an excuse." He drew even closer to her. "Let me have you too. We're all going to die now. So let me have you too." He grabbed her wrist and whispered, "We're all going to die. This is my dying wish. Let me have it." The pale man grabbed her by the shoulders and tried to draw her into a kiss.

She didn't understand his words, but his actions were clear enough. Disgusted, she pushed him away, and his upper body slammed against the bulkhead. A white ray just missed his head. She crouched, then slowly stuck her head out again and resumed her observations.

Something hard touched her shoulder. She looked back.

The pale man was aiming a gun at her.

"I'm going to have you. It's my last wish. We're all going to die soon. So let me have you."

He was sweating and trembling. Still holding his gun to her face, he jumped on her and started kissing her. His damp, sweaty hand groped her breast. She fell backward from his weight.

Her sword slung from her shoulder was now underneath her back. The pale man was heavy and sweaty and smelled wretchedly. She managed to get ahold of the end of her scabbard, pull it out, and stab him in the side with the blunt end. He let out an "Oof" and let himself be rolled off her, dropping his gun in the process.

She quickly got up and unsheathed her sword. When the pale man got up and made to come after her again, she pointed the sword to his throat.

He paused. He raised his arms and slowly started to back away. She kept her sword raised as her eyes followed his retreat. At a certain distance, he turned to run. A white ray sliced him neatly and soundlessly in half. He didn't even have time to scream as the two halves of his body tumbled into the white dust.

She quickly ducked behind the bent bulkhead. Another sweep of rays passed around her.

She stayed by the bulkhead, her face buried in the soft, white sand. When the rays stopped, she got up, sheathed her sword, and slung the scabbard over her shoulder. And she picked up the gun the pale man had dropped.

The white spaceships had vanished. She was surrounded by corpses and destruction. The smell of burning and blood and death filled the humid air. She looked around for survivors among the rubble.

The white aliens had been precise and thorough in their killing. Most of the bodies were either sliced in half or decapitated or had large holes bored through them. She found a woman who had lost an arm, groaning among the wreckage, and managed to get her out from under a pile of bodies, making a tourniquet with the clothes of one of the deceased to staunch the bleeding. She tried to get the woman on her feet, but the sight of her own sliced arm made the injured woman collapse onto the ground in sobs. She managed to get her on her feet again, almost hugging her in the process.

A gunshot. The arm of the woman she was supporting spasmed, then went limp.

She looked behind her. A gray uniform was pointing a gun at her.

Still holding onto the other woman, she aimed with her right hand and fired at the leg of the gray uniform. He fell and kept shooting, but all of the shots missed. Before he could raise his gun again, she fired.

Carefully, she laid the woman down. After making sure the gray uniform was dead, she came back to the injured woman. Who was now also dead, having been shot in the back and head.

She closed the woman's eyelids. She walked up to the gray uniform again. Roughly, she took up his rifle and slung it on her shoulder with her scabbard. After grabbing his flask and taking a long drink of water from it, she started stripping his body of ammunition when suddenly, she met his lifeless eyes with her own, giving her the impression that he was still looking at her.

She stood. She aimed at him with the gun the pale man had left behind. Until the magazine emptied completely and made a clicking sound with every pull of the trigger, she fired again and again.

*

A sharp scream, from a woman. She snapped out of her daze, lowered her gun, and ran to where she heard the scream come from.

She kept tripping over the bodies strewn about, and it wasn't easy following the screams through the red-black dark. The screams would be muffled, then pierce through the air, clear as crystal. She ran and ran.

There was a gray uniform atop another gray uniform. Ready to kill them both, she unsheathed her sword. But just as she was about to plunge her sword through both of them, she saw the face of Light Green Skirt, who was the one on the bottom.

She threw her flask on the ground and grabbed the gray uniform on top by his collar, who was perplexed at first and reaching for his gun in the next moment, but she was quicker with her sword—she stabbed him in the neck.

The blood spurted like a fountain. He struggled, and the effort made the blood splatter even more. She dropped the man, and using her procured rifle, shot him in the head.

She helped Light Green Skirt to her feet. Light Green Skirt's face was swelling from being beaten, and her nose was bleeding. Her tunic was torn and her waistband loosened. She could barely breathe with rage as she kicked the gray uniform's body several times, tears streaming from her face, and had to be urged to drink the remaining water in the flask and replace her torn tunic with the dead man's.

"I don't know where Tumina is," sobbed Light Green Skirt as she changed her tunic. "A white blast passed by right in front of me, and I ducked, and she wasn't there when I looked up again. So I was looking for her when this … trash …" Light Green Skirt sobbed harder and began kicking the man's body again.

"He's already dead. Let's go find Tumina." She tried to calm her down and gave Light Green Skirt the machine gun from the dead gray uniform. Still sobbing, Light Green Skirt accepted the weapon. Giving the body one last good kick, she let herself be led away, still wiping tears and blood from her eyes.

*

Not far along, they came upon some gray uniforms. They looked like they were searching for survivors among the bodies. A skinny, tall prisoner whom she didn't know approached them, limping and with his hands raised above his head. The gray uniforms asked the prisoner something. The prisoner nodded and pointed somewhere. The gray uniforms shot him. It was too sudden for the prisoner to even scream. He was shot a few more times, ensuring he was dead, and his killers continued on in the direction he had pointed.

"What are they doing?" she whispered.

"Looking for survivors," Light Green Skirt whispered back.

"But why are they killing them?"

"Who knows why."

She thought of how the injured woman she had been helping up was shot by a gray uniform. They weren't going around killing the injured, thinking they were useless. They were killing any prisoner, injured or not.

The tall and skinny prisoner had pointed somewhere—he had probably indicated there were more prisoners in that direction. She had to get there.

Just as she was about to turn, Light Green Skirt grabbed her elbow and whispered, almost inaudibly, "Behind."

She looked behind her.

Two gray uniforms were aiming their guns at them.

—Surrender your weapons.

The gray uniform's voice came out distorted and mechanical through his helmet's speaker.

She tossed her handgun in their direction, then the rifle. Light Green Skirt surrendered her machine gun as well.

—*Is this all?*

She nodded. Knowing that the Imperials didn't consider their swords as weapons, she didn't surrender her scabbard.

But the gray uniform confounded her expectations.

—*Drop your sword. It is a weapon.*

Slowly, she unslung her scabbard. The strap dropped from her shoulder down her arm.

—*Hurry up.*

She pushed Light Green Skirt to the ground with her scabbard and fell, grabbing the young man's gun from her inner thigh. A bullet grazed past her shoulder. She ducked and began to fire at them, hitting one on the shoulder and leg. It was hard for her to aim because of the kickback. The gray uniform shot in the shoulder and leg gritted his teeth and aimed for her head. She closed her eyes and kept shooting. The gray uniform fell backward. A bullet whizzed over her head.

When she opened her eyes, Light Green Skirt was chopping off one of the hands of the other gray uniform with the red sword and piercing him in the stomach for good measure. As the gray uniform lifted a gun with his intact hand and aimed it at Light Green Skirt, the woman shot him in the head. He fell back dead, the sword still in his gut.

Light Green Skirt, panting, retrieved the sword and wiped the blood on his trousers, and handed it back to its owner, who picked up her scabbard and sheathed it.

She counted the number of bullets left in the young man's gun: three. She strapped it back in its place on her leg.

Red Sword

"Where did you get that?" Light Green Skirt asked.

She shook her head.

The two women gathered the guns and bullets that had belonged to the dead soldiers and made their way to where the tall and skinny man had pointed, even though she was convinced that any survivors must be dead by now.

By the time they got to where the tall and skinny man had pointed, four gray uniforms were pointing their guns at three survivors. Blithely, Light Green Skirt unslung the machine gun she had taken from her rapist and shot at the gray uniforms.

The machine gun was powerful and its kickback intense. The first two shots felled one of the gray uniforms before the kickbacks made Light Green Skirt lose control of where she was shooting and the bullets scattered through the air.

She noticed the man was among the prisoners.

The gray uniforms turned and trained their guns at her and Light Green Skirt.

—*Surrender your weapons.*

It was the same twisted machine voice.

She raised her gun at them instead, and the gray uniforms took aim.

Light Green Skirt was quicker. The machine gun wasn't precise, but it was strong. A flurry of bullets sent the three gray uniforms and three prisoners ducking for cover.

Before the gray uniforms could get up again, the man also joined in the attack. She ran toward the man. One of the gray uniforms tried to get up but she shot at him, hitting the ground near his elbow as she wasn't good at running and shooting, but she did get him to drop his gun. Quickly, the man picked up this gun and fired.

He was good with the gun, fast and accurate, shooting all three gray uniforms while still lying there on his stomach. By the time she made it to him, he was already sitting up with the other two prisoners, sighing with relief.

"Are you all right?" he asked her and Light Green Skirt.

She looked back. Her friend was bleeding right above her pelvis.

"A surface wound," the man said, reassuring.

"Hurts," Light Green Skirt complained. The man ripped off a relatively clean part of one of the dead gray uniforms' garments, balled it up, and handed it to her.

"Press down on it."

She did, grimacing.

"Are you all right?" he asked the bearer of the red sword this time.

"Tumina," she said in lieu of a reply. She and Light Green Skirt launched into an explanation, but before they could get very far, white spaceships rose out from the red-black horizon.

She saw them first.

"Duck!"

They all ducked as the soundless rays of death rained around them.

The survivors could not stay in the same place. The white rays swept the ground, burning the bodies of the already dead, eliciting an occasional scream when they finished off the merely injured. The survivors scattered, following the places where the beams had already passed through, but there was no real place to hide except underneath the singed corpses, which was vile beyond imagination but the only way to survive. As she hid like that, she witnessed right in front of her a ray slicing through a pile of three bodies and realized this was not an ideal cover either. She needed more protection …

And just as she was thinking this, raising her head a little to look around her, a dark shadow flew overhead.

It was a swathe of black against a red-black sky, but she recognized it immediately. The shadow slowly descended, letting out an ear-splitting shriek at the white spaceships as it attacked.

One of the many white spaceships began to crash, spewing smoke. The black shadow breathed fiery plasma. The rays of the white spaceships turned from the prisoners on the ground to the Imperial attack vessel, which fought back with more plasma.

More black shadows descended. Another white spaceship fell out of formation, smoking all the way. The black shadows concentrated their plasma at it, the sound and even the heat of the blasts reaching where she was. She buried her face in the ground and protected her head.

The shrieking and the heat continued for a long time. Her face buried in the ground, she thought of Light Green Skirt and the man and Indigo Skirt, wherever she may be. The white chicks pecking at her body, the way the chewed-up corpses fell from the bird's wing onto the white ground. The woman who looked like her with her shredded back and her exposed bones and organs, her unfocused eyes. She didn't want to die here. She had no idea where she was or why she was here, or even who she was, but it didn't matter if she were fake. She wanted to live.

The shrieking stopped. Cautiously, she loosened her grip on the back of her head and looked up. There were still black shadows above her, but the white spaceships that had filled the horizon were all gone.

Slowly, she got up to her hands and knees. She called for Light Green Skirt.

"Atung!"

Among the pile of corpses, an arm creeped out and waved. Keeping herself low, she crept toward her.

The attack vessels above began to descend, making loud sounds and emitting great heat. She stood up and ran.

With Light Green Skirt, she watched the Imperial attack vessels land in the red-black night. There were seven of them in all.

"A lot," murmured Light Green Skirt.

She didn't know what that meant. Gray uniforms had tried to kill the survivors. When the uniforms were going about in twos and fours, she and Light Green Skirt could take them on. But if there were, say, seven gray uniforms at once, even the machine gun would not be enough for the two of them to fight off.

Light Green Skirt grabbed her hand.

She squeezed back.

The attack vessels lit their spotlights and swept the area. The lights from the seven ships were enough to make the ground eerily bright. Neither she nor Light Green Skirt could look at it for too long.

She squeezed Light Green Skirt's hand again, not letting go. Bullets and plasma could rain down on them at any second. There was nowhere to run from death now, should it come for them.

Some of the blinding lights went out. There were no bullets. She was puzzled by this, but also increasingly frightened, as she watched one of the vessels descend.

An airlock opened and a ramp extended down. Someone came out.

She let go of Light Green Skirt's hand. Light Green Skirt, surprised, called out her name. She didn't respond. She began walking toward the person coming out of the airlock. She ran.

The young man, or the man who looked like the young man, saw her.

"Chrisna!" he shouted, calling her name.

Just then, a woman who looked just like her came out of the hatch onto the ramp as well and stood next to the young man.

Double Helix IV

They themselves did not understand the white planet completely.

Human cloning, the electronic manipulation and creation of human consciousness, and the transplanting of such consciousness to other organisms were illegal throughout the galaxy they had left behind, much less their home planet. Their high command had therefore conducted their memory transplanting and human cloning research in secret, sending the researchers disguised as space explorers to the white planet. Aside from the high concentration of dust in the atmosphere, the mass, volume, gravity, and atmospheric makeup of the planet were similar to their home world. More importantly, no one knew about this planet on their home world, the star it orbited not even registered. When they discovered there was water on the planet, they quickly landed next to the white and opaque river and began their experiments. They sent out the black birds from the spaceship's lab to the white sky, and when they returned, they extracted the birds' memories to collect information about the planet and transplanted them to the next generation of birds. Until the birds learned to flock together and kill them and attack the lab with their beaks and claws.

The human beings knew of no future. They thought the flock of murderous black birds would be their greatest threat. They never dreamed white aliens would come looking for them on top of that.

Their urgent distress call spread out indiscriminately into space. They hadn't foreseen their call would be received by those who were not of the Empire. Just as they were about to send out the first human clones from their labs, the white aliens who had intercepted their distress call landed on the other side of the planet. They explored the terrain and collected information, adapting fast. More white aliens landed, and they built a permanent base and extracted resources. They did not look like they would leave anytime soon.

The Imperials took this as a declaration of war. The white planet was theirs—they had come first, they had staked their ground. And their manufactured humans, with their transplanted memories, were about to help them take their first step to creating a self-sufficient community on the alien world.

The Imperials refused to back off. Not only had they come here first, they could not let it be known that they'd engineered lifeforms and created humans and transplanted human memories.

The Empire finally replied. It was short and as predicted. A different expedition force would create more humans for them in support, and the original deployment were being ordered to produce more clones as well.

This was, of course, the same answer to their initial situation with the black birds, and their current situation was different. But the Empire's larger intent was clear. They were not to abandon the white planet, no matter what happened. They had to protect their new colony. By order of the Empire.

And so the war began.

7. *Young Man*

The woman who looked just like her, who wore the gray uniform of the Imperial forces, held up her gun at her.

"Don't kill her," said the young man to the woman who looked like her, gently pressing down on the barrel of the gun so she would lower it.

"Why not?" she protested. "Isn't it the rule to kill the previous stock when we're restocking?" She spoke fluent Imperial.

The young man grinned.

"There's still a use for her."

He gestured to her, as if calling forth a pet dog.

"Chrisna. Come here."

She hesitated. The young man grinned and gestured again.

"I said. Come. Here."

She didn't. She had never seen this sight before, the young man wearing a neat gray uniform and smiling at her in arrogance. This was not the young man she had known and loved.

"Huh. I guess I'll go down then." Taking his time, he came down the ramp. As the woman who looked like her tried to follow, he gestured at her to wait. "I have some business to take care of with her. Stay here."

"But security—"

He held up his hand again, stopping her flawless Imperial.

"It's all right. Go inside."

His tone was gentle but it was an order. Looking dissatisfied, the woman who looked like her gave a curt nod and went back into the attack vessel.

The young man, or the man who looked like him, slowly walked down the rest of the ramp. She couldn't help staring at him. He looked exactly like the young man she had loved. She was scared that a white ray would come out of nowhere and slice him in half, to the point where she began to tremble. But nothing happened to the young man, who stepped forth onto the white ground in the red-black darkness and leisurely approached her.

"That spaceship you stole from the monsters? We're going to that now," he said.

Her face drained of all blood, and cold sweat beading her forehead, she continued to stare as he smiled and slipped his arm into hers as if they were going on a date.

"I will tell you everything you want to know on the way."

He then turned to Light Green Skirt and the man, who had come running as soon as the ship had landed and were now standing nearby, and smiled at them as well.

"Tell your friends to come with us. We've got lots of room, and the more the merrier."

His arm still linked in hers, he started to walk.

Not knowing what else to do, she followed.

Red Sword

"So. What have you found out about the white monsters?" the young man asked as they walked arm in arm. As if she had promised to tell him before they had parted. It was really his tone, not his question, that made him hard to understand as she continued to stare at his face. He met her gaze and laughed at her.

"The white aliens, I mean. You've been fighting them, correct? With swords? And you visited their little spaceship, yes?"

When he mentioned "swords," he made swishing motions in the air, and for "visited" he made his fingers mime walking.

"You met their leader deep inside the spaceship, did you not? What was that like?"

With "leader," he mimed a crown being placed on his head. She was beginning to find his mocking manner off-putting. The young man continued to use his hyperbolic, exaggerated miming to talk to her.

"We do need your help. They're beginning to understand the severity of the situation over there and are about to attack, so we've got to get ready to counterattack. The biggest battle yet, I think. Our last, decisive battle."

He whistled, a tune she had never heard before. He seemed to find her hardening expression amusing.

"Ah, I suppose you don't recognize it? Because it's a song from an age much later than when you lived."

"Who are you?" the woman asked.

The young man stopped. He bowed a little, slipped his arm out, cradled her face with both hands, and looked directly into her eyes.

"What you really want to ask is, who are *you*?"

His smile was obscene now. She didn't answer.

He relinked their arms and continued walking as if they were taking a stroll.

"You're a clone," he said. "That bastard you liked, he was a clone, too. You're all clones."

"And you? Who are you?" she asked again.

He burst out laughing. "Me? I'm the clone of a clone of a clone!" He gestured wildly in the air with his free arm. She stopped walking.

"Laughing, I won't. Who are you? Who am I?"

"You're nothing. You're a clone, a fake. *Nothing.*"

That obscene smile. He added, "Well, since you *are* nothing, I suppose you can sort-of-kind-of-perhaps-maybe say that you can be whoever you want …"

The stolen white spaceship wasn't far from where the battle had been. It looked like it had been moved a little farther in from the riverbank. The sight of its white gleam in the midst of the red-black darkness made her skin crawl.

The young man was still prattling on with his nonsense, making more noise than sense. Ignoring his words, she unstrapped the young man's gun from her thigh and pointed it at him. The young man's smile remained as he raised his arm and exaggeratedly backed off, saying, "Hey, hey, careful there, we still have the last battle to save humanity left …"

As he was about to sing again, she interrupted him.

"This, you gave me?"

He didn't answer her right away but smiled and tilted his head. She asked again.

"Kill the Imperials, did you say?"

"I told you to kill the Imperials? Me?" He shook his head vigorously, the rictus still on his face.

Red Sword

"Bullets, you gave me? Why?"

There was a sob in her voice. So many things to ask, but her Imperial wasn't fluent enough, and who was this horrid creature standing in front of her, and why was she feeling more confused the more he spoke to her?

He stopped shaking his head. "I want to die," he explained. The corners of his mouth were still upturned, but his face seemed heavier, harder. "I want to completely, irrevocably die. Like any original human, like any ordinary, normal human used to."

She couldn't understand. But she also couldn't grasp which question to ask in order to get the answer she needed.

The young man gently wrapped his fingers around her hand that was pointing the gun.

"Let's do this." He drew her to him. "Win this war. If you can banish those white monsters, I'll give this planet to you and your friends."

"The planet?" She felt confused. "Imperials? Soldiers?"

"Just kill me. Everything will fall into place." His grin was so wide it was like he was telling a funny story. "Win the war, banish the white monsters, kill me, take the whole planet. It's a perfect plan!"

She shook her head. "I want to go home. I don't want to kill you. I don't want to kill anybody. I just want to go home."

The young man laughed.

"Why don't we discuss the details at a later date and talk about the white monsters for now. Because that seems to be a matter of higher priority, wouldn't you agree?" He shushed her as she was about to say something and gestured to Light Green Skirt and the man.

"My friends, please come. You need to hear this as well."

And as if they had just shared a juicy secret, he smiled and winked at her.

The hatch of the white spaceship opened without a sound. She followed the young man inside, remembering when she had been dragged in as a captive. Nervous, she looked back at the man and Light Green Skirt.

The inside of the white spaceship was dim and the machinery not working. It was quiet. Knowing his way, the young man led them through various twists and turns into a room that had many panels and no doors. Under the many panels and displays, he slid out something round and flat that looked like a stool and sat down. Bidding the others to stand around him, he began his story.

The point was that it was a territorial dispute, according to the man, who interpreted for the young man. The white planet did not belong to the white aliens. It belonged to no one. The white aliens themselves did not come there to settle on it. They only wanted its resources. Most of it was a certain ore they needed for their communications equipment, and sometimes the fur and leather and bones of the occasional black bird, which were converted for industrial purposes.

"And we need resources, too." He listed the names of some ores she wasn't familiar with. "Those white bastards don't even want to live here, and it doesn't belong to them in the first place, so why should we spend our good money on buying it? We're both descended from Earth and therefore brothers in a way, so why can't they let us mine a little and share in the wealth?"

"Brothers?"

The young man laughed and waved his hands as if waving away her confusion. "Sorry, sorry. I really should make an effort to be precise. Let's say far-flung relatives. Because we're not white-blooded like those bastards are and we can hear."

"Relatives?" she repeated. "Descended from Earth?"

"It was such a long time ago that it's hardly even worth talking about, but yes, technically they descended from Earth." He looked almost smug relating this. "They left Earth and settled in this galaxy a long, long time ago. It's been about a thousand or a thousand and five hundred Earth years since they cut ties, so they might as well be natives to this galaxy now."

"A thousand years?" She turned to the man, wanting to verify if she had heard right. The man looked as disconcerted as she felt, glancing at her and then the young man.

"You heard right. I know you're only pretending not to understand Imperial. You understand everything." He winked again. "Over a thousand years, in any case. Maybe almost two thousand? Since those white bastards left Earth." His more artificial smile, the one where just the corners of his mouth turned upwards, returned as he spoke more slowly. "Your people went extinct even longer before that. You're just the clone of a clone of a people who died a long time ago."

He stared into her eyes until he was sure what he had said registered with her.

"There is no home for you to go back to. You've never had a home to begin with." He looked at the man and Light Green Skirt. "Oh, and the same goes for your friends."

"Really? You didn't know?"

The young man seemed amused, looking at the three of them, asking again and again.

"You've never felt your memories didn't quite feel like your memories? That your pasts and presents were mixed up? That your childhood memories and the times you find yourselves in didn't, ah, quite match? Well, I guess none of you have lived a long enough time to feel anything about the past."

"Our memories are fake?" Light Green Skirt asked, butting in.

The young man made a grand, sweeping gesture. "Congratulations! You are the first to come to that realization."

Light Green Skirt ignored his gestures and demanded, "Then this war, those white monsters, how do we know they're real?"

"Oh, it's just you who are fake. The rest is real," he said, all smiles. He thought for a moment and said, "Well, I guess I'm fake, too. I guess I'm the fakest of the fake." He gave another meaningless wink at the woman with the red sword and said, with a serious face, "But aside from that, it's all real. This planet, the white monsters."

"Then why did you kill the survivors?" Light Green Skirt's voice sounded like it was about to crack. "Don't you need them in a war?"

"Because they're almost all dead anyway, it's neater to just kill off the whole lot and send out a new set." He laughed. "Think about it. Would you even care about fighting if you saw a bunch of people who looked like you walking around in your side's uniform? You'd all turn into philosophers, wondering who you were and why you existed."

Light Green Skirt glared. "What happened to Tumina? Did you people kill her?"

Red Sword

"Your girlfriend? I don't know. As I keep telling you, those white bastards are not on our side, they don't listen to what I say." He tilted his head left and right. "Well, if you feel that sore about it, I can make you a new one."

Light Green Skirt lunged at him, but he was quicker, jumping back from his stool just in time as the other two grabbed her arms.

She whispered, "You can't kill him. He may know where Tumina really is and isn't telling you."

The strength left Light Green Skirt's body, and they let go of her arms.

She noticed Light Green Skirt was slightly shaking, so she gripped her hand firmly.

"No, I really don't know where your girlfriend is," said the young man, having heard her whisper. "But I can guarantee you that you'll like your new girlfriend clone just as much. That's really the amazing thing. Whether they have their memories or not, the people who like each other always end up liking each other. Like you and your clones liking me and my clones," he said, pointing at her. "Or him and his clone liking you and your clones," he said, pointing at the man. "It's a good thing one of those men died pretty quickly. Otherwise, there would be this tiresome love triangle on top of having to fight this war."

"Why did you bring us here?" Light Green Skirt's voice was cold. "You wanted to bore us with your taunts?"

"Oh good, finally someone wants to get to the point. Excellent." He looked around at them one by one. "I'm going to take you to the white monsters' headquarters. You need to kill their leader. Then, you'll be free."

"What are we going to do with this freedom?" said Light Green Skirt. "You said yourself we've no home to return to?"

"Just because you have nowhere to return to, it doesn't mean you won't be free." He looked thoughtful. "The only real life you've actually experienced is the time you've had since arriving on this planet. Isn't that a great place to start?"

He got to his feet.

"Great, so let's go kill some aliens."

"Why us?" she asked, urgent. "Us, three people, few. How can we kill leader?"

"Because of all the versions we've experimented on, you three had the best results." He turned and pressed the panel in a sequence.

The interior brightened. So much so that she squinted.

"Ah, sorry, sorry, this is what happens when you have glitches in transplanted memories." He laughed and touched the panel again. The light dimmed to tolerable levels.

He suddenly bowed deeply over the panel and for a long time said nothing as he rubbed his forehead. Light Green Skirt gave her a look.

He straightened up and barked, "All of you, get out. I need to concentrate on controlling this thing."

They stood there, uncertain of what to do.

"I said get out! I don't know what you do when you prepare for battle, but go do that."

Light Green Skirt was the first to comply. Still taken aback by the about-face, the man followed.

She was the last to leave the control room. When she took a backward glance, she saw the young man take a small bottle from his pocket and empty its contents into his mouth and rub his forehead.

The control room entrance that had no door suddenly disappeared behind the expanding translucent membrane of the wall, which right before her eyes turned a solid white.

"I'm going to kill that bastard," said Light Green Skirt after the door closed.

"Now?" she said.

"Why not?" Light Green Skirt's rage was palpable.

She took a step back from her. "No, I mean, do what you want."

The man next to her asked, "We don't know how to fly this thing."

Light Green Skirt glared at him.

She said, in a small voice, "He's right."

Light Green Skirt glared at her. "Fine. But we're just going to go into the white aliens' headquarters, just like that, because he asked us to? What are we going to do when we get there?"

"Do we have any other choice?" said the man quietly. "If we kill him now, the spaceship will crash. If we crash-land the spaceship, we'll be stranded somewhere we don't know anything about. And even if we somehow convinced him to take us back, would the Imperials welcome us? Did you forget they just killed their old stock so they could have a new set?"

A silence.

"So no matter what we do," murmured Light Green Skirt, "we die."

The floor vibrated, startling them, and they made to flee. But when it vibrated one more time, the membrane hiding the control room entrance dissolved; the door opened. The floor vibrated again.

"Sorry about that," the young man shouted from the other side, "I turned on the PA and the floors got all jiggly. The white monsters have a weird language. Anyway, we're arriving in seven minutes, get ready to fight!"

They could see him cheerfully giving them a wave. The translucent membrane covered the entrance again and turned solid.

She unslung her red scabbard from her shoulder. She held it in her hands and stared at it for a moment.

"Whatever we end up doing," she said grimly, "let's live through it."

In a cabinet next to the airlock. The three found several sets of the white armor the aliens wore in battle. They each selected whatever was closest to their size.

She didn't know how the white aliens put them on, but because the gloves got in the way of handling the other items, she saved them for last. She couldn't see a thing when she lowered the translucent visor on the helmet, making her grope everywhere for her gloves, dropping them in the process.

"Three minutes to landing!"

It was impossible to find the gloves, but just as she was about to take off her helmet again, someone pressed her hand. She looked up to see the faint outline of the man's face out the visor. He hadn't put on his helmet yet.

He said nothing. He simply held her hand in his firm grip.

"Two minutes!" shouted the young man from the control room.

She could feel Light Green Skirt looking in her direction. But

Light Green Skirt said nothing and turned her head.

The man slowly put on her gloves for her. First her right hand, then her left. He then put on his own gloves.

Lastly, he held out his helmet to her. She put it on for him, clicking it into place.

"One minute!" screeched the young man. He let out a yelp.

The white spaceship soundlessly landed in the aliens' base.

She picked up her red sword and slung the red strap over her shoulder.

"Let's go," she said softly, knowing full well that she was inaudible to others inside her helmet.

The young man was saying something, but she couldn't hear him anymore. She was alone in a whitish world, cut off and silent.

The airlock opened.

Her sword on her shoulder, her grip on the strap not as tight as it could be because of the glove, she and Light Green Skirt and the man took their first step into the heart of enemy territory.

Light Green Skirt said nothing and turned her head.

The man slowly put on her gloves for her. First her right hand, then her left. He then put on his own gloves.

Lastly, he held out his helmet to her. She put it on for him, clicking it into place.

"One minute!" screeched the young man. He let out a yelp.

The white spaceship soundlessly landed in the airlock.

She picked up her sword and slung the red strap over her shoulder.

"Let's go," she said softly, knowing full well that she was inaudible to others inside her helmet.

The young man was saying something, but she couldn't hear him anymore. She was alone in a soundless world, cut off and silent.

The airlock opened.

Her sword on her shoulder, her grip on the strap was as tight as it could be because of the glove, she and Light Green Skirt and the man took their first step into the heart of enemy territory.

8. *Infiltration*

During her short walk down the ramp from the airlock, she learned a few things about their armor.

She had to stop in the middle because she couldn't see a thing outside of her visor. As the other two descended without her, she rubbed at her visor with her hand. It didn't get any clearer. But a few hard wipes made it suddenly go transparent. When she rubbed again, it went opaque.

The man looked back at her. Seeing her fiddling with her visor, he walked back up and tapped the front of her helmet twice. The visor turned transparent.

The man moved his lips. She couldn't hear anything. She shook her head.

The man indicated the front of her helmet with his index finger. He spun it.

"Face?" she shouted from within her helmet.

The man nodded. He pointed at his helmet, then at hers. Then he mimed shooting a gun.

She understood. If their faces are seen through the transparent helmet, they would be exposed.

But she needed to see in front of her. She began fiddling with the helmet, pressing down with one hand and swiping the visor with another. The world darkened a shade. Not as dark as when she first wore the helmet, but the light certainly became less intense. She tried it all the way—she could still see out, but the outside of her helmet was now opaque.

She tapped the man's helmet and demonstrated for him the same gesture. He nodded, understanding. Light Green Skirt had also paused, watching them.

She quickly went up to Light Green Skirt and showed her how to make her helmet one-way as well. Light Green Skirt gave a start when it happened and tried out the settings herself.

At the bottom of the ramp, a group of white aliens were sliding toward them. She quickly tapped Light Green Skirt's shoulder, who turned her outer visor to opaque, hiding her face.

The white aliens were riding on some kind of thick, white panel that floated. It stopped in front of the ramp. The ground under the three of them sank into the same shape and size as the panel, and the panel neatly landed inside the newly formed depression.

There was no time to be astonished at this mode of transport. They were soon surrounded by white aliens. The ground vibrated. Light Green Skirt was about to whip out a white wand.

She stopped Light Green Skirt, stretching out her hand. Her other hand quickly groped about her own leg, looking for the communications device she'd seen the aliens employ. Their language was incomprehensible, but she had to at least pretend to try.

The ground vibrated again. She found a button and pressed it.

—*. . . the crew of 378ŁĘ28ΠΘ?*

Red Sword

She heard it. To be more precise, she felt the meanings in her brain. It was a different sensory experience from hearing words, but she understood their question clearly.

—Answer. Why do you not answer? Are you the crew of 378ŁĘ28ΠΘ?

Fascinated as she was by this new experience, they were repeating their question, and she needed to answer.

She pressed the button and thought, as clearly as possible in her own language, *We need to see the leader.*

The ground vibrated.

—The Commander? Why is that? Are there more survivors? Are you injured?

Success. She took her hand off the button and pressed it again.

Just us. We are not injured. We need to see the Commander.

—Good. But you need to go through quarantine first. We will summon the medics.

This was a complication. With no time to think it through, she held up the scabbard she was carrying.

This, I need to show them this. There is something important the Commander must know about this object. It is about the movements of our enemy. She was making things up as she went along.

But the white aliens were adamant.

—Medical protocol comes first. We shall be endangered if we are exposed to the diseases of the aliens. We do not know what this object is, it needs to be sterilized.

She almost laughed at the term "aliens." But the white aliens were dead serious. They had no intention of going against protocol.

It was all too obvious what would happen when their medics

stripped off her armor and their identities were exposed. "Soldiers will be executed when the fog lifts." That's what the leader of the ship they had eventually taken had dispassionately said that day.

When the aliens attack, the entire base will be in peril. I must meet the Commander now.

She said this with as much authority as possible and stared at the white alien officer in front of her, trying to glean a clue about their thoughts.

After a silence, they finally answered.

—*Fine. We will report you to the Commander. We will go directly to headquarters.*

The ground vibrated. The three of them, surprised, looked down. The floorspace around them lifted slightly from the ground, becoming a panel again, and began to move. It made her think of the story from her childhood about a magic carpet.

Whose childhood that was, and whose memories, if it was indeed a memory of a non-clone instead of herself...

The ground vibrated again.

—*You are sure you are not injured? Even a small injury presents the danger of infection. It must be treated.*

This was the white alien behind her, a different one from the one she had first spoken to.

We are fine. We have no injuries.

—*Even if you are not injured, you will be hungry and tired. I am glad you all came back alive. Once you have seen the Commander, you must eat and rest.*

Thank you, she almost replied before she stopped herself. The white alien made a light gesture with their hand that she didn't understand.

There was silence after that. Light Green Skirt held her hand.

She showed Light Green Skirt how to work the communicator on her leg. Light Green Skirt was startled when the ground vibrated, but she soon nodded in understanding.

She turned to the man and pointed to the button. He nodded, he had figured it out. He tapped his leg.

She turned her gaze to the aliens' base they were passing through. There was one thought that persisted inside her like a fishbone in her throat.

This is not my war.

The white aliens were no monsters or invaders. If anything, the wrong side here was the Imperials. The white aliens were the ones whose territory had been breached.

She was not an Imperial. If it weren't for the deal proposed by the young man, she had no reason to attack them.

We will summon the medics. Medical protocol comes first. The white aliens were rational, and they seemed to have a system of rules in place keeping it together. *I am glad you all came back alive. You must eat and rest.* The words made her heart ache. She was only a prisoner on her own side, and while the other prisoners could say they were glad she had come back alive, they couldn't provide her with food or rest. To actually be given the dignity of a community, to be respected and protected and given her fair share of resources and taken care of—these were things she had experienced for the first time, and it was through the enemy.

What if they were to negotiate? The best thing would be if no white aliens had to be killed and the man and Light Green Skirt and herself lived. She tried to think of a way.

She had no time. The magic carpet panel carrying her party

arrived at its destination. A depression appeared in the floor and the panel sank neatly into it. The three prisoner-spies were escorted to a white staircase with a black landing.

The floor vibrated. She pressed the button on her leg.

—*The air circulators function. You can take off your helmets.*

The white aliens had already taken off their helmets. She stared at their pure white hair, pure white skin, their irises that were so dim they were barely distinguishable from white, and the shocking black points of their pupils.

The floor vibrated. It was the man speaking.

—*We did not go through quarantine. We shall keep our helmets on.*

Surprisingly, there were no objections to this.

The stairs began to move upwards in silence.

The floor vibrated again, and she hurriedly pressed her leg button.

—*As you did not go through quarantine, regulations dictate you must stand at a distance from the Commander. The item you bring her shall also be subject to basic sterilization before it is handed over. Understood.*

The stairs took them to a white wall. One of the aliens pressed it and communicated with the interior. The opaque wall turned translucent and then melted away. The inside was a not-very-wide room, and behind a desk-like object sat the thin and old white female she had seen before.

The escorts gestured for the three to enter. She did, and the man and Light Green Skirt followed.

As soon as Light Green Skirt stepped into the room, the white wall reappeared. The white aliens surrounded them, wands ready, and the three of them instinctively raised their hands.

Their wands were confiscated, and one of the white aliens took the red sword.

As she worriedly watched them handle the sword, the floor vibrated again, startling her. She pressed her leg button.

—Who are you? And what have you done to the crew of 378ŁĘ28ΠΘ?

Before she could answer, Light Green Skirt charged at the white alien in front of her and smashed her helmet into their exposed face.

A battle ensued.

She knew from experience that the armor did not protect them against the white rays. She had to avoid the shower of rays somehow, and at the same time, steal back one of the weapons and approach the Commander.

Easier said than done. The rays seared her back, shoulders, and limbs, and they seemed to be fighting an infinitely replenishing number of white aliens. She grabbed a wand and shot at whatever she saw that moved.

The wall behind the Commander's desk turned transparent and opened. More white aliens emerged. Two of them stood next to the Commander, who stood up, which made her nervous—but the Commander did not flee. She simply gazed at the three prisoners fighting for their lives.

The three of them were captured and disarmed. Their helmets were taken off. The thin, white Commander looked intently at their faces.

The floor vibrated. Once, twice. The Commander was speaking, but without her helmet on, she couldn't understand what it was she was saying. She was reeling from the pain of her burns and so exhausted that, if it weren't for the white aliens propping her up, she would've collapsed on the ground.

Another white alien came up to her and touched a part of her armor that made it freeze in place. Her arms and legs were fine, but she couldn't move the armor and was stiff as a tree. They did the same thing to Light Green Skirt and the man.

The white alien doing the freezing came back to her and grabbed her head. Thinking her throat would be sliced, she struggled with all her might, but once the alien stuck something to her temple, they let her go. Light Green Skirt and the man were given the same temple sticker.

The floor vibrated.

—*You two are familiar.*

The sentences came into their minds clear as day. The Commander was handed the red sword from one of the white aliens flanking her.

—*What is this object? Why are you trying to give it to me?*

She didn't answer but stared at her sword. She had to take it back somehow. Somehow . . .

The floor vibrated.

—*Are you the best soldiers the gray ones have?*

Gray ones. She burst into laughter. Here they were, thinking of them as the white aliens, and the white aliens were thinking of them as gray ones. When they were both descendants of Earth, children of the same blood, giving each other designations according to the color of their respective uniforms—it was too much for her. Not to mention that she was not an Imperial and therefore not a gray uniform, nor was she their best soldier. The fact that every word of what the Commander had said wasn't true made her want to laugh even more. She gritted her teeth, struggling to hold it in, but that wasn't enough as she began to tremble from the effort, and tears rolled down her cheeks.

—*What's going on?*

The Commander rose from her seat, looking alarmed.

—*Disease?*

That single word made the white aliens holding onto her let go and take several steps back. This situation made her laugh even more. She suppressed it as much as she could, shaking in her stiffened armor, falling over like timber, the sticker falling off her temple.

"My companion has fallen!" the man shouted in Imperial. "She will die if you just leave her like this! Let me go! Please!"

The Commander said something incomprehensible, and the white aliens holding onto the man pressed something in his shoulders and his armor unfroze. He quickly ran to her and unfroze her armor in the same way. Carefully, he lifted her to her feet.

She was crying and convulsing with suppressed laughter as she looked into his eyes. Shifting her gaze, her eyes met Light Green Skirt's.

Light Green Skirt turned her head and bit off the cheek of the white alien standing next to her.

The white alien grabbed their face with both hands. White blood dripped on the floor. Their mouth was open as if to scream, but there was no sound. The other white aliens holding onto Light Green Skirt abandoned her to take care of their friend, pushing her to the ground.

The man leaped to Light Green Skirt's side, blocking the attacking white aliens with his body, and unfroze her armor as well.

Light Green Skirt spat out the white flesh of the alien and grabbed the wand of the one that was lunging at her. She fired everywhere. After enough of them had fallen, she went straight for the white Commander.

Before the other white aliens could stop Light Green Skirt, they were attacked by the other two, giving Light Green Skirt time to shoot at the white Commander, hitting her in the arm and making her own shot glance upward, searing Light Green Skirt from rib to shoulder.

Light Green Skirt screamed in pain but continued to charge at the Commander, colliding into her and making her fall backward in a tangled pile. Light Green Skirt slammed the Commander's hand against the table leg, making her drop her wand, and just as she was about to shoot her, the Commander punched her in her shoulder wound and tried to strangle her.

But Light Green Skirt was screaming like a beast and operating under pure rage. No matter what the Commander tried, nothing seemed to affect her. When the Commander managed to get on top of her and strangle her, Light Green Skirt grabbed her scabbard and forcefully stabbed the Commander with the blunt end.

The Commander fell, holding her own neck. Light Green Skirt drew her sword as she got to her feet and stabbed her again. As white blood spurted, she punched the Commander again and again and again.

The white aliens stopped their attack and stared at their Commander being pummeled by Light Green Skirt.

Red Sword

She was the first to come to her senses. Pushing aside the white aliens, she ran to Light Green Skirt's side, who continued to scream and scream as she punched the Commander.

"Atung," she kept saying. Light Green Skirt did not listen to her. "Atung, stop." She grabbed Light Green Skirt's arm. Light Green Skirt struggled against her grip. She forcefully hugged Light Green Skirt's shoulders.

"These things killed Tumina," screamed Light Green Skirt. "These things killed Tumina, these things killed Tumina! Let go! I'll kill all of them!"

"Atung, she's already dead. Stop it."

Light Green Skirt convulsed in her arms one more time before the strength left her and her eyes stared down at the white face of the Commander. The Commander was covered in white blood, and her features were so mashed it was impossible to recognize her. She lay unmoving on the floor.

"She's already dead."

Her sword and red scabbard were lying there beside the body. She quickly wiped the blade against her armor the best she could and sheathed it, then slung the scabbard on her shoulder.

Shaking, Light Green Skirt stood up. Her friend helped her.

The man rushed to Light Green Skirt's other side. They both kept murmuring Light Green Skirt's name as they carefully crossed the white room. None of the white aliens attacked them.

When they stood in front of the wall with the exit, one of the white aliens opened it for them. The three of them left the room without a word.

The last thing she saw of them when she looked back was the Commander's body being carried away somewhere.

Once they were down the moving stairs, they ran. Light Green Skirt seemed to have come to her senses. But as the shock wore off, the Commander's ray blast that had seared her was sending her into an agony of pain, and the other two had to practically drag her along between them. They threateningly waved their stolen wands at any of the other white aliens they came across—while the white aliens in the room had stopped their attack when the Commander fell, they had no way of knowing whether the ones outside would do so as well.

But the aliens didn't attack. All the way to the white spaceship where the young man was, no one tried to approach them. They simply stared, startled.

She didn't have the time to think about why. Light Green Skirt was about to collapse from pain. She didn't know where the white spaceship was—all she could do was follow whenever the man shouted, "This way, that way."

Finally, the white spaceship. The ramp came down, and she and the man dragged Light Green Skirt up to safety.

The first thing they did was to make sure Light Green Skirt was seated in a comfortable position. The airlock closed, and the whole spaceship began to vibrate.

"What is it?" She stared at the man, frightened. Maybe the white aliens were being ordered to attack, to capture, or kill Light Green Skirt, who had killed their leader.

"They're being ordered to leave the planet," the man said. He still had the small white sticker on his temple. The vibrations continued. "They're saying headquarters has been attacked and their commander was killed, that it's dangerous here. That they can't guarantee the safety of the civilian contractors and are closing the quarry for the time being." The strong vibrations abruptly ended.

The young man popped out of the control room.

"They've ordered a moment of silence for the dead Commander!"

He looked overjoyed as he smiled that rictus grin of his, looking at each of their faces.

No one answered him. The young man's voice grew louder.

"You did well! Excellent! You're now free! Aren't you excited? Why aren't you dancing? Shall I dance for you instead?" He raised his arms over his head and began to spin and spin.

She was beginning to notice there was something off about him, especially his eyes. There were red spots around his eyes, which were bloodshot, and his pupils seemed a little unfocused.

"Get us out of here, please," said the man with some heaviness. "Our friend is hurt. She needs care."

The young man didn't stop dancing. He continued to leap and dance and shout. "Friend! Ooh, your friend! She's not interested in you at all! She likes women, you see? But friend! How wonderful! You can't sleep with her, so instead, she's your *friend*!"

"Go now," she said. She looked directly into his bloodshot, unfocused eyes.

The young man stopped dancing. He lowered his arms and shuffled back to the control room.

"Tumina," whispered Light Green Skirt, wrapping her arms around the burn wound that crossed her upper body. "Tumina."

She put an arm over Light Green Skirt's shoulders and let the injured woman lean into her as she sobbed and cried out for her lover.

The spaceship took off, light as a feather into the air, slipping away from its original home of the white aliens to where the Imperials in their gray were waiting.

She patted the sobbing woman's back as the man simply sat by the two and gazed at them in silence until Light Green Skirt, exhausted, fell asleep.

The spaceship shook violently. Light Green Skirt was startled awake. She tried to stand up but the pain of her injuries made her grab her shoulder and waist and give a short scream as she fell back down.

"What happened?" Light Green Skirt whispered, gasping in pain.

"I don't know. I'll report back," she replied.

When she stood up, the spaceship keeled over.

*

The three humans fell sideways and slid across the floor. Light Green Skirt grabbed her elbow, cursing under her breath.

She asked, "Are you all right?"

Grimacing, Light Green Skirt nodded. "I bumped against something."

The man was rubbing the back of his head.

"Are you all right?"

"All right?"

They asked each other at the same time. She carefully stood up.

Red Sword

"I'll be back."

The spaceship turned almost perpendicular.

*

The aliens' gloves and boots had their uses, but crawling up a smooth floor was not one of them. She had to carefully grab at the various devices on the floor-turned-wall to move around, and some of the handles and protrusions on these devices would give way in her hand, not designed to bear such weight, or spark and shock, or make another device pop out from somewhere. The control room, only a few paces away, seemed almost beyond reach.

The doorway was open at least, and she grabbed the doorframe and peered over the edge. The young man was lying on the wall in a strange position. The angle of his arm suggested something was broken.

She managed to heave herself over into the room. She called out the young man's name.

There was no answer. She carefully approached him, crawling across the wall.

He was in a seizure. His face was covered in red, swollen splotches, and one of his eyelids was closed and the other open as he stared into nothing. His mouth foamed.

She called out his name. He didn't reply. She carefully put her hand on his face.

The young man moaned, more foam escaped his mouth, and his unbroken arm and both legs flailed as he spasmed. The foam from his mouth turned red.

He sounded like he was choking. Carefully, with her fingertips, she moved his chin so his face went sideways, and the red foam started coming down the side of his face. He was still having a seizure, but the painful sounds he was making ceased.

"What's going on?"

She turned around. The man had come inside the control room, carefully leaning against the floor.

"What's wrong with him?"

"Don't know." The urgency of the situation hit her. "Spaceship, stop it. We fall. We die."

The man climbed up the perpendicular floor and grabbed the pilot's chair, using it to hoist himself in front of the panels.

"Stop! We fall! Die!" she shouted.

"I know!" he shouted back.

Half-mounting, half-hanging onto the control panel, he tried some buttons but nothing happened. The tilted spaceship did not right itself.

"I don't know how to do this!" he shouted. "It won't listen to me!"

The spaceship began to shake the walls and floor with a new desperation. Large, black symbols flashed on the panels.

The man quickly came down from the pilot's seat, slid across the floor, and extracted her grasp on the young man, gripping her wrist.

"We are going to crash," he whispered.

He pulled her into an embrace.

The spaceship crashed.

9. *Mothership*

The sound of metal tearing. An echoing pounding. A wedge of light split through the darkness. She dropped down to the yellow-lit white sand and dust, which entered her nose and mouth. Coughing, she stood up. Her whole body ached.

The first thing she thought of was her sword. It was lying next to her, covered in white dust, but upon inspection was intact. She reflexively slung it.

Then she saw the man lying nearby. She carefully shook his shoulder.

"Wake up," she whispered in her language. "You mustn't die. Wake up."

The man slowly opened his eyes. He raised his head a little and looked at her. Then he lay back, stared up at the red-black sky, and mumbled something in his language as if to complain.

"Hurt?" she asked in Imperial.

The man screwed his eyes shut and slowly sat up. "Are you all right?" he asked.

She nodded. But the moment she nodded, her head, neck, and shoulder hurt, and she regretted answering with a nod.

The white spaceship was wedged into the white earth, with

the airlock half-buried. Evidently, the Imperials, who did not know how to control the white aliens' spaceship remotely, had decided to cut a hole through the hull instead. The two of them had been the first to fall out, and now the gray uniforms were pulling the young man out of the wreckage. Gray uniforms with green medical armbands came running to administer care to the young man and take him to the gray patrol ship.

But what of Light Green Skirt?

She quickly got to her feet.

"Atung!" She ran about the wreckage, calling out Light Green Skirt's name. "Atung!"

There she was, just visible through the airlock that was open a crack in the white sand. Light Green Skirt was covered in dust and blood, the white sand turning red around her.

She tried to force open the hatch. The man came running up to help, and they both managed to get the opening wide enough to pull her out. But Light Green Skirt's eyes would not open, and she was limp in her friend's arms.

She half-carried, half-dragged her to where the medical gray uniforms were administering to the young man. Not because she expected them to help, but she had to do something. She was desperate. The man followed her, worrying for her.

The gray uniforms grabbed her and twisted her arms around her back, forcing her to drop Light Green Skirt and fall on her knees. She screamed.

The young man, lying in the gurney, raised his head. His face was still covered in swollen red lumps, and his hand made the same arrogant gesture of summoning a pet dog. Immediately, the woman who looked like her put her face near his mouth, and he said something to her before dropping back, exhausted. The gray uniforms lifted the gurney and swiftly took him into the patrol ship.

The woman who looked like her gestured to the gray uniforms and said something quickly in Imperial. The gray uniforms let go of her and grabbed Light Green Skirt by the arms, forced her to her feet, and started to drag her away.

She tried to stop them, but the woman who looked like her said, "They're taking her away to treat her." She smiled a twisted smile, where the corners of her mouth went up but her eyes were full of hate. "Consider yourself lucky."

The woman who looked like her then said something to the remaining gray uniforms and followed the young man into the patrol ship.

The gray uniforms grabbed her and the man and dragged them back into the ship as well.

Inside, they were thrown into separate, dark cells in the belly of the ship once more, the gray uniforms locking the doors and shoving food and water through smaller doors before locking them as well, leaving them in the dark.

She didn't want to eat. She pounded against the door, demanding to be told whether Light Green Skirt was all right. There was no one outside, and the silence of the dark corridor did not answer her demand.

The man knocked on the wall between them.

"You have to stop that," he said. "Eat something and rest. That's the only way you'll be strong enough to save your friend."

She collapsed on the floor and drank some water. But she

was too worried to eat. The severity of Light Green Skirt's injuries, how her blood had soaked the white sand around her. Memories of Light Green Skirt and Indigo Skirt's bodies rolling around on the back of that bird. The other woman who looked like her, with her three remaining fingers on her blackened hand. The look of death on her face when they finally made it out of the bird's pit, the eyes without focus …

She hugged her scabbard. She slammed her whole body against the wall. Once. Twice.

"Calm down!" the man shouted from the adjacent cell. "That's not going to work! You'll only exhaust yourself!"

She kept slamming herself against the wall. She wasn't doing it to get out of the small room. She was doing it because the narrow darkness was pressing down on her, and the helplessness it brought was unbearable.

When she was about to slam the wall again, the room shook. She lost her balance and fell on the floor, almost letting go of the scabbard. The tray with the food went flying against the wall.

The room shook again, and there was a familiar humming coming from the walls and floor.

They were launching.

She slung her scabbard and stood up. The floor was shaking so much that it was hard to keep herself upright, but that didn't matter. She pounded the door with her fists.

"Where are we going! Where is Atung! Where are you taking me!"

No one answered her. Not even the man in the next cell.

The flight didn't last too long. She kept pacing inside the small space of the cell. Her anxiety and helplessness and her inability to disperse either feeling was making her rage spike. Her worry over Light Green Skirt and where they were being taken and what was awaiting them when they landed once more was making her dread the future more and more. She had fought the white aliens and killed the Commander, just as the young man had told them to, but their reward had not been their promised freedom but this cell and this tiny darkness. The thought made her hug her sword and slam her whole body against the wall.

The shock of this physical contact at least stopped her thoughts for a second or two. Her shoulder hurt, but once the pain ebbed away, the thoughts would start again. The young man was dead but not dead, the man was dead but not dead, Light Green Skirt wasn't dead but had died somewhere, and who knew how many Indigo Skirts had died or were alive at any given time. She kept thinking of the bodies on the bird, of the woman who looked like her. She had no idea who she was anymore. She'd been told her memories were fake. She was probably fake as well. Now that she knew the home in her memory didn't exist anymore, the "freedom" she had kept in her heart as her ultimate goal was now meaningless. She wanted to delude herself into thinking that it still existed, that freedom was real, that the life she wanted was hers as long as she worked hard enough for it. But she had seen, with her own eyes, people who should've stayed dead come back alive, people who did not remember dying. There were no more reasons to be skeptical. Herself, all the people she believed were her friends, and all the prisoners were just copies of other people, with no pasts and no futures. Their lives were all a lie. She slammed her forehead on the wall.

"Don't do that," the man said. "If you hurt yourself seriously, you'll be able to do nothing. You have to keep it together for your friend."

Instead of answering, she punched the wall hard. Her hand hurt. The pain was consoling, which made her hit the wall again and again.

"I know," the man said. "I know, too."

His saying that, for some reason, made her feel relieved. She stopped hitting the wall and curled up in a fetal position with her back against it. Hugging her red sword. She held her aching fist with her other hand.

"I'm right here," the man said in a low voice, "and I'll always be here."

She leaned her head on the wall. Imagining the man on the other side was doing the same thing. She listened to every movement he made. Because even when everything was fake and a lie, this moment at least was completely true.

The patrol ship landed, shaking the dark cell. She got on her feet.

The small door opened. Gray uniforms gestured to her. She came outside.

The soldiers didn't open the man's cell. They were taking only her.

"Where are you taking me?"

The soldiers didn't reply. A soldier grabbed her right arm, another her left. She tried to resist.

"Where are you taking me!"

Wordlessly, they dragged her away.

They were no longer on the white planet but inside another spaceship. The corridors were long and wide, and everything was dark gray, light gray, or bluish or yellowish gray, and everything from the doors to the walls to the ceiling was much larger than the patrol ship she was familiar with.

The room the gray uniforms took her to was also larger than any room she had seen on the patrol ship. The woman who looked like her was waiting inside. After shoving her in, they saluted to the woman who looked like her and left the room.

She glared at the woman who looked like her. She got a sneer in return.

"Don't worry. Someone who remembers is asking for you."

"Someone who remembers?"

The woman who looked like her didn't explain. She used the same arrogant gesture reserved for pet dogs to get her to come closer.

Defiantly, she didn't budge. The woman who looked like her sighed.

"If it were up to me, I would've had you killed a long time ago." She clucked her tongue. Then she said the name of the young man.

"He's asking for you."

The woman who looked like her made a *follow me* tilt of her head.

So she followed her.

The young man wore a thick bandage wrapped around one arm and lay in a bed. His face was pale and his eyes were bloodshot, but the red blotches on his face were gone. He looked almost glad to see her. He then looked at the woman who looked like her and said, "You can leave."

The woman who looked like her seemed perturbed and was about to object, but she thought better of it and left the room without a word, dissatisfaction on her face. The door closed behind her.

"Come here."

She didn't move.

"What happened?" she said instead. "Where is Atung?"

"Atung? Oh, the one that likes girls?" There was a kind of malicious glee in his eyes. "I don't know, actually. I assume she's somewhere here, getting treated."

"Where is here?"

The young man laughed. "Here? It's the mothership. You don't remember? Well, I guess there's no reason why you should."

"Mothership?" she said, confused.

The young man grinned. "They only have emergency care on the patrol ship. Nothing that can treat the brain from having had too many memory transplants. This is our headquarters and our mothership. We have everything we need here."

"Why does your brain malfunction?"

The young man's face changed. The taunting smile and the hostile glare died down, and for a second he almost looked like the young man she had once known.

"Come here," he said. She stood where she was, staring at him. He asked again. "Come closer. I have something to tell you."

His voice was soft, and his face looked much like the young man she had loved. She went up to his side by the bed.

"You haven't forgotten our deal?" he said. "If you chase away the white monsters and kill me, I'll give you this planet? It's now your turn to kill me."

What? He was asking her to kill him? Of course, it would be easy enough. He was lying in a hospital bed without the use of one of his arms. But she was thinking of the gray uniforms who had brought her here. Of the woman who looked like her. The young man was clearly someone of importance among the Imperials. If she killed him now, it was more likely she would receive a death sentence than her freedom.

"I'm not telling you to kill me now," he continued in a low voice, "I'm going to die anyway. But those bastards are going to take my memories and put them in the next me."

Using his uninjured arm, he took off something that had been hanging around his neck and placed it in her hand, wrapping her fingers firmly around it. Something hard. His fingers were cold. She was too surprised by his contact to resist.

"This is a key," he said.

It was a small, thin panel, smaller than her palm. Blue-green, translucent, and smooth, with dots and symbols stamped in gold on the surface. She stared at it in her palm. She couldn't even guess as to how it could be used.

Taking the "key" out and giving it to her seemed to have exhausted him. His face very pale, he whispered, "Kill my clones. All of them. Then kill me." His voice was getting smaller. "Quickly. Before I die. Before they shove me into another clone."

He raised a pale hand and pressed a device next to the bed. The door opened and the woman who looked like her entered. Just as she grabbed her arm to drag her out, the young man whispered, "Let her go."

The woman who looked like her stopped in her tracks and glared at him.

He whispered again, "Don't lock her up. She proved herself. She'll be a great help. Respect her."

The face of the woman who looked like her hardened. But she let go of her arm.

The pale young man closed his eyes, sighed, and turned his head. The two women left the room.

As she followed the woman who looked like her, she requested the man be released as well.

"If you're letting me go, you have to let him go, too."

She spoke in her own language. Surely this woman who looked like her could understand without her having to resort to her awkward Imperial.

She added, "Where is Atung? Is she being treated? Let me see Atung."

The woman who looked like her stopped and turned around. She thought her Imperial counterpart was about to strike her.

But she didn't. She glared at her with rage-filled eyes and said, "Just because you were praised by the one who remembers, don't think you can go around having airs. You're a *prisoner*," she spat, "and until this war ends in victory, I suggest you don't forget it."

She wasn't perturbed by the words of the woman who looked like her. For if she was a prisoner, so was this identically looking woman in front of her. Something else was bothering her, however.

"What do you mean about this war ending in victory? We killed their leader. They abandoned their base. Haven't we won?"

The woman who looked like her scoffed. "That's just one of their outposts. We conquered it, but as long as their point of origin exists, they will come trying to get it back." A shadow fell over her gaze as she said with fierce hostility, "We are on our way to the white monsters' planet. *Victory* means conquering them completely."

Before she could say anything in answer, the woman who looked like her took out a small device and spoke rapid Imperial into it.

Two gray uniforms appeared. As if to make sure she was understood by her counterpart, the woman who looked like her spoke in measured, precise Imperial.

"Escort her to where the injured one is and take care of her. For she is a great warrior who will fight our battles for us."

The gray uniforms grabbed her arms, but with a lighter grip this time. The woman who looked like her turned and went back to the room where the young man lay.

Light Green Skirt lay on a gray bed inside another room, breathing regularly, seemingly asleep.

She took a careful look at her. The parts of her that were uncovered—her face and hands—were clean, and the various cuts and bruises seemed to have been treated. She felt relieved.

The door was flung open and gray uniforms tossed inside the man, who fell onto the floor. Not even closing the door, the gray uniforms turned and walked off.

The man groaned a little as he righted himself. She held out her hand and helped him up.

"What happened?" he said.

She explained as best she could. That they were on the Imperial mothership, on their way to the homeworld of the white aliens, and the Imperials, specifically the woman who looked like her, was intent on conquering this world.

She didn't say anything about the young man. But the man mentioned him anyway.

"What happened to the one who was flying the spaceship?"

"Hurt. A lot. Little bit, little bit. Dying."

"Then his promise to us was all for nothing? But we can't just keep getting dragged hither and thither by the Empire! Not to mention that the white aliens have more advanced weaponry than the Empire! Fighting against them on a wasteland of a planet is one thing, but to declare war against their homeworld? She's out of her mind. This is a suicide mission."

"Don't want war," she murmured. "Want to go home."

She looked at Light Green Skirt lying in front of her and sighed. A pair of gray uniform trousers by the bed caught her eye. While treating her, the medics had taken off her bloodied uniform and dressed her in a dark green loose garment. This uniform, filthy as it was, had been left crumpled in a pile next to the bed.

She picked it up. There was the long burn mark from the Commander's ray. She put it on over her tunic.

She couldn't do that for the trousers, so she began taking off her torn skirt.

"What are you doing?" the man said, quickly turning his back.

She didn't answer. She didn't understand herself the young man's request that she should kill all the clones, so she didn't explain it. But she was going to find out what he meant.

Red Sword

She still had the young man's gun strapped to her thigh. She took it out and stuck it to her waist, covering it up with the uniform top. The uniform had been taken from a male soldier and was a little too large for her.

She hesitated with her sword, but ended up slinging it on her shoulder again. The blue-green key the young man had given her was still in her hand. She put it in her trouser pocket. Once she was finished, she went for the door.

"Where are you going?"

She stopped the man from following her. "I'm going to end the war."

The man didn't understand. Acting on impulse, she drew him to her and kissed him lightly on the lips.

"Wait for me."

Leaving the confused man with Light Green Skirt, she left the room and began walking down the corridors.

The ship was large and there were few people. None of the gray uniforms passing by stopped her. A few gave her surprised looks, but she wasn't apprehended or questioned. When she was saluted, she saluted back. As she suspected, they thought she was the woman who looked like her. All it took was to tie up her hair in a knot and keep her mouth shut in a firm line and walk like she knew where she was going.

But the mothership was vast, much larger than the patrol ship. The more she walked around it, the more tired she would become and the likelier it was that she was discovered. She approached a man who had many decorations on his epaulets and said, "Where are the clones?"

The eyes of the man with the decorated epaulets grew wide, and he stammered slightly. She flashed him her blue-green key.

"The clones of the one who remembers," she spat out, imitating the enunciation and manner of the woman who looked like her.

The man with the decorated epaulets looked reassured.

"Follow me."

He led the way.

Through twisting corridors and lifts and more corridors, they reached the end of a long and dark hall where there was a door shut firm. The man with the decorated epaulets pointed at it and said, "Here."

He saluted and quickly walked away.

She approached the door. There was no handle, but a black depression about her chest height looked like the exact shape and size of her key. It indeed was.

The door silently opened.

She stepped inside.

The door slid shut behind her.

Another narrow and stuffy corridor. There were handle-less doors lining either side of it. No windows.

She went to the first door on the right. The doors had no handles but did have the black depressions. She keyed it open.

There were two large, semi-transparent, liquid-filled cylinders inside. She took a step closer and saw that each contained a man identical to her young man, lying naked and connected to various cables that snaked from their bodies to one of the walls of the room, which was covered in various devices and screens. There was no small and dark depression, but there was a groove that looked like she could insert the key into. When she did, a screen lit up with various symbols.

She didn't know how to read the Imperial alphabet. She simply chose a flashing red square on the screen and pressed it.

At first, nothing happened. But in the next moment, the wall filled with devices began to shut down section by section, and the several wavy lines on the screen became flat. In a short while, the blue-green key popped out of its slot.

She went to the other cylinder and did the same thing there. For good measure, she drew out her sword and cut the cables connecting the cylinders to the walls.

It was the same in the second room, the third room, and the fourth room. She tried hard not to look at the young men in the cylinders as she inserted the key into the slots and pressed the flashing red square for each of them, slicing the cables in each, locking the doors as she left with the key.

Her young man was there in the last, ninth room.

When the door opened, the stench made her almost throw up. She dry heaved for a while by the door, covering her nose and mouth with her sleeve. Then, she entered.

The room looked like it was full of corpses. Bodies missing various combinations of limbs. Everyone with the same face. The young man's face.

There was a wall of devices here as well, connected to a body that didn't have legs or one of its arms. When she approached it, the half-body suddenly opened its eyes. She stared down.

The body had been slashed from shoulder to hip, the slashed part lightly seared as if cauterized.

The young man called her name.

The key in her hand, she froze as she stared at the body.

"Chrisna," he said.

Slowly, she walked up to him.

"Chrisna," he said again.

She carefully bent down. She hugged the half of his body that remained.

"You came for me ..." he whispered in her ear.

She held him close to her and called his name. Again and again.

*

Gritting her teeth, she straightened up. Before she inserted the blue-green key, she looked back one more time at her lover. He gave her a gentle, exhausted smile. Instead of nodding, he slowly blinked.

She turned her back. She inserted the key. When the strange symbols appeared on the screen, she pressed the red square with no hesitation.

Until the squiggly lines turned flat and the machine returned her key, she kept her back to her smiling lover and stared at the letters on the screen that had no meaning for her.

Red Sword

As she began to sever the cables to his body, the room suddenly lit up with red light. All of the white, flat lines on the screen turned blood red. A fearsome siren issued. She quickly cut all of the cables and ran out the door.

The woman who looked like her was standing at the end of the narrow corridor. She could see gray uniforms behind her.

She thought of the gun she was hiding in her clothes. In one hand she held her sword, in the other, her scabbard. It would be too obvious if she were to reach into her uniform now. She would be dead before she could fire her gun.

The corridor was very narrow and long. Just about the width for one person. There wasn't enough room for all the grey uniforms to attack her at once.

She raised her sword at the woman who looked like her.

The woman who looked like her grinned. From an identical scabbard she was carrying on her back, she drew an identical sword.

They trained their swords at each other.

As she began to sever the cables to his body, the room suddenly lit up with red light. All of the white, flat lines on the screen turned blood red. A fearsome siren issued. She quickly cut all of the cables and ran out the door.

The woman who looked like her was standing at the end of the narrow corridor. She could see grey uniforms behind her.

She thought of the gun she was hiding in her clothes. In one hand she held her sword, in the other, her scabbard. It would be too obvious if she were to reach into her uniform now. She would be dead before she could fire her gun.

The corridor was very narrow and long. Just about the width for one person. There wasn't enough room for all the grey uniforms to attack her at once.

She raised her sword at the woman who looked like her.

The woman who looked like her grinned. From an identical scabbard she was carrying on her back, she drew an identical sword.

They trained their swords at each other.

10. Mano a Mano

"You're going to die either way. Put down your sword and surrender," said the woman who looked like her, smooth as cream.

"And you're going to die by my own hand," she answered.

That twisted smile again. The woman who looked like her moved her scabbard to her right hand, sword to her left, pointing the scabbard and holding the sword over her head.

She was confused. This was a method she had never seen before. Picking up on her reaction, the woman who looked like her made that taunting smile again.

"Your memories are my own. Everything you know, I know. Everything."

As she spoke, the woman who looked like her began to approach, pointing the scabbard at her, making her take a step back in surprise.

"I! Know! Everything!" the woman who looked like her screamed as she brought her blade down with force.

She jumped away in time. The sword identical to her own only nicked her forehead, the space between her eyes, and the tip of her nose. The resulting blood trickled down to her lips and she tasted salt.

The woman who looked like her smiled in satisfaction. She shook off the blood on her blade and raised her sword above her head again, pointing her scabbard at her opponent.

Whereas she stood holding her sword with her right and her scabbard with her left. The woman who looked like her advanced half a step. They looked like mirror images of each other.

"Huh. You think all you have to do is imitate me?" The woman who looked like her began to laugh.

She attacked, not even waiting for her to end her laugh. She feinted a strike with the sword in her right hand while in the last second jabbing the woman who looked like her in the sternum with her scabbard in her left hand.

But the other woman was faster. She turned to avoid the blade from above and struck her left wrist with her scabbard, making her drop it. The woman who looked like her kicked her scabbard behind her and took another large step.

"I thought I told you I know everything you know? Surrender now, and I'll let you die more comfortably."

As she spoke, the woman who looked like her switched her sword to her right hand and her scabbard to her left. She raised her scabbard over her head and made to go for the neck.

She managed to swerve away just in time. The hall was too narrow to escape. She had to turn her body sideways. She could parry the last attack but just barely, as it glanced off her shoulder, ripping the seam of the gray uniform she wore and making her bleed, soaking her arm.

The woman who looked like her didn't even break a sweat. She was slowly shaking off blood from her blade.

She looked behind her. She was almost at the end of the corridor. There was nowhere left to run.

The woman who looked like her noticed her realizing this. "I told you that you were going to die anyway," she taunted. "It's not too late to surrender. I'll give you a nice, clean death, here and now."

She subtly centered her weight, adjusting her grip on the sword and scabbard, squeezing down on her left ring and little fingers. Her body turned into a straight line when seen from the front and back.

"Are you meditating?" said the woman who looked like her with a scoff, making little circles with her sword tip.

She stayed centered.

With a roar, the woman who looked like her charged.

Not moving back an inch, she plunged her blade forward, knocking the other woman's blade sideways, the upturned blade grazing her right wrist.

Her opponent's sword tip had been aiming for the artery on her wrist but instead had only grazed it and cut her forearm. The woman who looked like her shook the blood off her blade again, mocking her with the motion, which splattered blood all over the wall next to her. The sight caught her attention, as if it were a piece of art she was admiring.

She put strength into her grip, centered herself once more, and pointed her sword tip at the other woman's neck.

"Yes," said the woman who looked like her, "it's a good idea to think about your life a little before you die. Now there's nowhere for—"

She had taken a step forward, ducked, and pierced her sword

right into the belly of the woman who looked like her, the tip protruding out her back.

It had been ridiculously simple. The woman who looked like her gawped in surprise and looked down at her stomach.

She pushed her sword in to the hilt and twisted it, stepping close to the woman who looked like her. The latter woman stared at her, eyes and mouth wide.

Quickly, she let go of the plunged sword and grabbed the young man's gun hitched inside her uniform and shot the woman who looked like her in the temple.

As the body fell, she extracted her sword and bent down to wipe the blade on her vanquished foe's uniform. She sheathed the woman's sword that looked like her own in the scabbard that looked like her own. Then, as she walked to the exit, she picked up her own scabbard that the dead woman had kicked and sheathed her sword.

These two swords slung over her shoulder and the young man's gun in her right hand, she walked down the corridor to the gray uniform standing at the door.

"Take me to the one who remembers."

The gray uniform in front of her hesitated.

"Now!" she shouted.

He stepped aside. She stepped out. The gray uniforms surrounded her.

Still armed, she slowly began to walk, escorted by the gray uniforms all around her.

When she stepped in the room, the young man was sitting on his bed. There were other people there as well. Light Green Skirt and Indigo Skirt turned to look at her.

Red Sword

"Tumina!" she shouted, running up to Indigo Skirt. "Tumina! You're alive!" Overjoyed, she made to hug her but Indigo Skirt was stepping back, her eyes wide. Light Green Skirt stepped in between them. The two woman were glaring at her with suspicion.

That's when she noticed a woman in loose, dark green robes standing a little farther away. She looked identical to Light Green Skirt and wore a sling on her left arm, her bandaged left shoulder slightly visible at the neckline of her robe. This other woman was shaking her head at her, distress in her eyes.

She took a step back. Light Green Skirt and Indigo Skirt also took a step back, holding onto each other.

She turned to the smug young man sitting on the bed and shouted, "What's the meaning of this!"

He seemed amused at the situation unfolding before him. The sight of his pale, smiling face made her remember the other young man in the secret room in the belly of the mothership, the half-alive, half-dead young man persisting in the stench. The last, painful smile he had given her to the end. She raised her gun at him.

Indigo Skirt and Light Green Skirt darted to the other side of the room, and the gray uniforms at the door raised their guns at her. The woman in the dark green robe held up her free hand and tried to stop her.

Only the young man seemed unperturbed.

"It's fine. Lower your guns," he drawled at the gray uniforms.

She didn't move, and so, neither did the soldiers.

"Chrisna," he said, speaking her name. She didn't move. "Chrisna, lower your gun. Let's talk." His smile faded from his face.

The same eyes. The same look that she had loved. It hit her hard.

Slowly she lowered her gun. The soldiers did as well.

The young man gestured at the gray uniforms to leave. When they hesitated, he barked, "I said I needed to talk to her! Get out!"

They stepped out of the door. Indigo Skirt and Light Green Skirt tried to follow, but the door shut in their faces.

"You two stay," the young man said coldly.

Holding hands, they looked at each other and the young man, trapped. Their frightened faces made her heart ache.

"What are you doing to us!" she shouted at the young man.

"Well, your friend said she wanted to find her girlfriend," he said casually. "I figured she's already dead and wanted to make her a new one, but that clone over there insisted on following."

"I didn't ask for that," growled Dark Green Robe, her voice crackling with fatigue and rage. "I want *my* person. I didn't ask you to make me another one."

He only grinned his mocking grin.

By the way Dark Green Robe was holding onto her shoulder wound, she could tell the woman was barely keeping herself on her feet. Every word she spoke was from inhuman effort.

"I am not that woman. We are all different people. You can't just make a person and have them take the place of another."

As if he'd heard a good joke, the young man laughed long and hard.

"What idiocy. Such primitive sentiments. You better get your friend to sit down. She's going to bust her stitches like that."

She wanted to say something in defense of Dark Green Robe,

but she really did look like she was about to faint. She quickly went to her side and helped her to a chair. The two women by the door still had suspicion in their eyes, but their fear seemed to dissipate a little at the sight of her helping Dark Green Robe.

She went up to the young man on the bed and stood before him.

"I killed all your clones." She took out the blue-green key and tossed it on the young man's bed. "As you promised, give us our freedom."

He picked up the key and held it up to her. "Keep this. You might need it sometime."

She didn't take it. "Who are you? Why did you do this to us?"

He lowered the hand offering the key. He looked up at her, the mirth fading from his face.

"I didn't do this to you," he said with a heavy voice. "This is the way of the Empire. They clone individuals from extinct peoples and use them to invade and colonize other planets and steal their resources and technology. They make those civilizations extinct and clone them for more prisoners to invade more worlds. Everyone in this spaceship is a clone. We are all clones and property of the Empire."

"The soldiers? Everyone?" She couldn't believe it. "Like the prisoners?"

His smile was wan. "The distinction between prisoner and soldier is arbitrary. Depending on what memories you get grafted, you become a prisoner or a soldier. Sometimes, you get the wrong memories transplanted and that creates a bit of a mess, but the mistakes can always be killed off and a new batch put out."

"But why? Why have prisoners and soldiers? Why not just all soldiers so everyone would be loyal to the Empire?"

"It's more convenient for the clones to fight each other and distrust each other. They keep each other in check that way." His voice was almost devoid of emotion now. "A very small number of people understand how the Empire really works. The word 'empire' sounds complicated, but it's really just a handful of people controlling everyone else like puppets. If the clones were only soldiers and not prisoners, there may be a rebellion and the Empire would collapse quickly."

"Then who are you?" She could not stop asking this question. "Are you the emperor of the Empire?"

He laughed. Not a mocking laugh this time, but a sad laugh.

"I'm the one who remembers."

"What is it that you remember?"

"Everything."

The Empire survived by stealing. The decision-makers in the imperial core had created a system where, instead of passing on knowledge and traditions to the following generations, they delighted in finding useful resources or technologies and making their owners extinct for them, and moving on to the next target. Because the Empire's technology and civilization came from stealing from and destroying other people, they were ignorant of the proper uses of these technologies and knew nothing of what they meant or how they would impact their future. When they obtained the ability to clone humans and insert fake memories, the powerful of the Empire were simply satisfied they could produce an infinite number of soldiers and slaves. And of those manufactured slaves, the few that happened to withstand multiple memory grafts without going insane ended up with the role of managing the vast amounts of information needed to control the many sectors of the Empire.

"They thought that elevating us above the other clones would keep us loyal to the Empire, but even all the ones that remember are slaves in the end," he said. "We're just the oldest slaves of all."

Human lives were finite, and it was extremely rare to find one who had the capacity to maintain large stores of memory for an extended period of time. The young man's brain excelled in the storage and retrieval of memories, and once this was proven to the Empire's decision-makers, they decided it would be easier to clone the young man instead of managing different kinds of "ones that remember" in the transmission, extraction, transplanting, and retrieval of information.

This fact, of course, had to be kept a secret to the slaves, in other words the prisoners and soldiers. They had to continue having their false hopes and goals so they would stay true to the Empire's purposes and aims, sacrificing themselves for families and loves that haven't existed in centuries. The young man was the model they sent in to spy and collect information on the male clones, while a woman spy was sent in to do the same for female groups, a woman model whom the Empire considered the ultimate feminine experience, that of a mother deeply attached to her children.

"Isfobeddin," she murmured. "So her children never existed in the first place?"

The young man averted his gaze from her. "They existed. Once upon a time. The Imperials don't know how to make new memories. They can only edit existing ones."

"But her children don't exist anymore?"

The young man bowed his head.

She thought of Isfobeddin's final moments. The desperation in her voice as she called out the names of her children who were long gone.

The young man massaged his temples. He looked up at her again. His face was even paler and his eyes a little bloodshot. His pupils were losing their focus. Closing his eyes, he pressed his palms against the sides of his head.

"Kill me," he said. He opened his eyes and stared into her eyes again. "Kill me, and if you ever see me again outside of this room, kill me again. Kill every single me."

The sight of his imploring stare made her think of the half-sliced young man as she held him in her arms. A suffocating stench of death had come from him. But he had whispered her name in her ear. In her memory, her real memory, his voice would forever be gentle and kind.

She did not want to kill the young man.

His pupils were losing focus again. He slouched, and slid onto the floor.

She quickly knelt and held him in her arms. He was trembling, his arms and legs beginning to shake. As his eyes began to move on their own accord, he whispered with the remainder of his control, "Kill me."

She held his gun to his head.

"Thank you," he said.

Just as she had turned her back on her lover, she turned her head away from him and pulled the trigger.

Red Sword

For a long time, she sat by the dead young man.

Something light touched her shoulder. Her head mechanically turned. It was Dark Green Robe, still holding her wound, awkwardly bending over in her discomfort and worriedly gazing at her. "Are you all right?" she asked.

"What do we do now? What are we supposed to do now?" she murmured back. Dark Green Robe didn't answer.

She looked down at the dead young man again. She could see the exit wound on the back of his head, but it was so small that it was hard to believe he was dead. An incredible amount of blood flowed out of his head and white fragments—of what, she didn't want to know—came out with it. The blood soaked her knee where his head rested. A smell of something she couldn't identify filled the air. She thought of the smell in the room that was filled with corpses. Of the gladness in the half-dead young man's eyes when he saw her.

Slowly, she rose. She turned to Dark Green Robe and said again, "What do we do now?"

Dark Green Robe gazed back at her. When she realized this was a real question and she wasn't speaking from shock, she replied, "I want to go back to the white planet."

"Why?" For this was a little surprising.

"Because Tumina is there."

She understood.

Dark Green Robe's knees buckled from pain.

She quickly grabbed her arm and helped Dark Green Robe sit down on the bed. Dark Green Robe smiled, exhausted. "I hate this bed. I hate this place. I want to get out of this spaceship."

"Where is the man?" She still didn't know his name.

"He's still in the room I was in."

"I'll go get him."

As she rose from the bed, Dark Green Robe grabbed her arm. "Isfobeddin," she whispered. "She's in the room with him."

She looked down, confused. "But she died?"

Dark Green Robe shook her head. "She's wearing a gray uniform and has a gun."

This short explanation was enough.

Helping her friend in pain lie down on the bed, she bent over Dark Green Robe and whispered, "Do you think this Isfobeddin will know where our patrol ship is?"

"I know."

She turned. It was Indigo Skirt who had spoken. "I don't know which patrol ship you took to get here, but I know where the patrol ships are. Take us with you." Still holding hands, the two women took a step closer to her.

She looked back at Dark Green Robe. She got a nod in answer.

"We'll take her there," Light Green Skirt said.

"Can you walk?" she asked Dark Green Robe, who nodded.

She touched the back of Dark Green Robe's hand. "I'll see you there."

Dark Green Robe nodded once more.

She stood up straight. She still had her two swords hanging from her shoulder and the young man's gun on her side. Her eyes caught the blue-green key on the bed. She picked it up and put it in her pocket.

As she left the room, she said to the women, "Be careful."

Then, she set out to find the man.

The man was sitting in a chair like a statue. Isfobeddin stood next to him, her back stiff.

She entered, and he got up from the chair, which made Isfobeddin raise her gun at him before she noticed who had come in.

Isfobeddin was indeed wearing a gray uniform. Her face betrayed no emotion, none of her old suspicious gaze or the cat-like, mocking grin of the other Isfobeddin. The sight of the woman still inspired fear, and somehow, this emotionless face made her seem even more fearful.

"Isfobeddin," she said with as much authority as she could muster. Enunciating as precise an Imperial as she could, she said, "It's me. Lower your weapon."

Isfobeddin dubiously gazed at her torn uniform and blood-splattered face and wounds. Of course, she had no way of knowing that the blood soaking her knee wasn't hers. It could only be hoped that Isfobeddin had not heard yet of the battle down in the guts of the ship.

The spy woman's gaze traveled up and down her body for a long beat. Then another beat.

Finally, she lowered her gun.

Inwardly, she sighed in relief. She spoke once more, in her clearest and most haughty Imperial, "We are going back to the base of the white monsters. Take us to the patrol ship."

"Haven't we already conquered it?"

This threw her. She glanced at the man. He looked equally thrown.

"A confidential matter," she said. "Take me to the ship."

Isfobeddin seemed to hesitate.

She gripped her own gun, not daring to breathe. She had one bullet left.

"Follow me," said Isfobeddin. Holstering her gun, she walked out of the room with her back still ramrod straight, her steps crisp and precise.

She exhaled without a sound and loosened her grip on the gun behind her back.

She gestured to the man. He immediately followed her out.

Down the long corridor and throughout the lift ride, Isfobeddin did not speak a word. During the lift's descent, she thought of the room hidden deep in the bowels of the mothership and the rooms where the young men had been locked away.

The lift stopped. The doors opened. She got off, then Isfobeddin, then the man.

Isfobeddin unhooked a small device from her belt and spoke into it. A distorted voice from the device spoke back something.

Isfobeddin said, "We're opening the hatch. Please give me the code."

She didn't know what Isfobeddin meant by code. All she had was the green-blue key the young man had given her. She took it out of her pocket and handed it over.

Her face not betraying an iota of emotion, Isfobeddin accepted it, flipped it over, and read aloud into the device the symbols stamped on the back.

The device gave another distorted reply.

Isfobeddin said, "It's done," and handed her back the key.

She casually took it from her, imitating Isfobeddin's stony expression, and slipped it back into her pocket.

There was a mechanical shudder, and one of the walls began to move.

"Follow me," said Isfobeddin, pointing to one of the patrol ships that were revealed on the other side.

Isfobeddin led them up to a ship, borrowed the key again to open it, and went up to the control center.

She sent the man up with Isfobeddin first and looked about for the three women.

"Chrisna," someone called out. The voice was so small it was hard to tell where it was coming from, but she soon spotted Indigo Skirt. She quickly gestured at her to come, which she did, supporting Dark Green Robe on one side while Light Green Skirt held on to the other.

Dark Green Robe hadn't been injured in her legs, but she had weakened considerably and couldn't move well. It was impossible for her go up the ramp on her own. The three of them half-dragged Dark Green Robe and half-carried her up.

Once they were safely inside, she left the injured woman in the care of the other two, and rushed up to the control center. Isfobeddin had finished her preparations for taking the ship out.

She said, "Go."

Nodding, Isfobeddin sat down in the control seat and touched various buttons. The airlock shut.

"Please enter the main cabin and put on your safety harness," Isfobeddin intoned.

She made to do so. She hadn't even known there was a "main cabin" as she had only known the prisoners' holding cells of the patrol ships and being transported like cargo in the dark. She didn't know where exactly to go but kept walking down a corridor until the man popped his head out of a door, and she went in.

This was the cabin. She finally took off the two red swords and laid them on the floor next to a chair before getting seated.

A familiar shudder—the patrol ship had launched.

It slowly floated out of an opened wall of the hangar and began crossing the immense darkness beyond.

Once the launch sequence was complete and the patrol ship was in cruise mode, she left the cabin to go looking for the women, going down to the lowest level first.

As she suspected, they were hiding in the cargo hold where the prisoners were usually kept. Dark Green Robe's face was pale, and she was in a cold sweat, her pain writ large on her face.

She gripped Dark Green Robe's cold hand. "Do you think you can walk? Let's find someplace more comfortable. We might find food and water somewhere."

The sick woman nodded.

The three of them managed to get Dark Green Robe to her feet, and they slowly walked her down the seemingly interminable corridor outside the cargo hold. When they went up some stairs, they had to pause several times to let Dark Green Robe rest.

They finally made it to the cabin. The man quickly got up to help them. They got Dark Green Robe to lie down and tried to make her as comfortable as possible, and the man left to find food and water.

She was sitting by Dark Green Robe's side. But Dark Green Robe didn't want her. She held her hand out to Indigo Skirt.

"Tumina," she whispered. "Tumina."

Red Sword

Indigo Skirt looked at Light Green Skirt. The latter woman nodded.

She let Indigo Skirt take her place, and Indigo Skirt held Dark Green Robe's outstretched hand.

"I'm right here," Indigo Skirt whispered.

"Tumina." Dark Green Robe gave a relieved smile.

Isfobeddin appeared at the cabin door. "Our course is set. We have about ..." Her voice trailed off when she saw the other women. She looked from Light Green Skirt's face to Dark Green Robe's identical one, then Indigo Skirt. Then her. Slowly, she pulled out her gun.

"Isfobeddin," she said, but Isfobeddin didn't reply. She was aiming her gun directly at the injured woman in the green robe.

"Isfobeddin," she said again, standing up. The gun moved to point at her.

"Don't move," said Isfobeddin. "Who are you?"

"Please put down your gun," she said. "I will explain everything."

"Shut up." Isfobeddin turned her gun back to Dark Green Robe. "Who are you all? Who!"

"Isfobeddin," she said again, and the point of the gun returned to her.

She held up her arms. Willing her to keep eye contact, she said, slowly, "Malenka. Levinok."

As she said the names of the children, she turned slightly so her back was directly in Light Green Skirt's face, and she moved her foot to slightly touch Light Green Skirt's.

"What did you just say," said Isfobeddin. It had been a whisper, but a tremble could still be heard.

"Your children, right?" she said as she moved a little again, eclipsing Light Green Skirt's right-hand side from Isfobeddin's perspective.

"You know where my children are?"

Isfobeddin's face, in a moment, had turned desperate. It was a very small change in her facial expression, but it was suddenly filled with surprise, suspicion, and fear, but also an ineffable sorrow.

She loathed using this trickery. It was cruel to manipulate Isfobeddin this way. But she had no other choice.

"Don't you want to see your children? Malenka and Levinok?"

She could feel Light Green Skirt slowly drawing out the gun from behind her belt.

"Do you want me to tell you where your babies are?"

Isfobeddin was staring at her in equal parts suspicion and desperation, wanting to believe more than believing. The tip of her gun started to go down.

Light Green Skirt kicked Isfobeddin's leg. She dropped to the floor.

Light Green Skirt fired the gun. The bullet went straight into Isfobeddin's forehead.

She knelt down next to Isfobeddin and took her pulse.

"She has to be dead," said Indigo Skirt.

She murmured, "I didn't want it to be this way."

"Who are Malenka and Levinok?" asked Light Green Skirt.

"Her children," she replied. "Her lost children."

11. Crash

The patrol ship silently crossed the black expanse.

The man had come running at the gunshot. He looked down at Isfobeddin's body. "What happened? Are any of you hurt?" He looked around at them, bewildered.

The women shook their heads. Reaching over Isfobeddin's dead body, the man gave Dark Green Robe some water and food, which Indigo Skirt took for her.

He began to carry out Isfobeddin's body. The woman helped. As they carried her down to the cargo hold, the man asked, "But what happened?"

She explained. He didn't react to her explanation but listened attentively.

She remembered how he had coupled with Isfobeddin. But that man was dead, as was that Isfobeddin. The man before her didn't know Isfobeddin, and the woman being carried out now didn't know the man. She thought of how the man had been shot in the head right before her eyes, of Isfobeddin's last moments as she screamed out the names of her children. A violent urge to vomit overcame her.

"Are you all right?"

She knew she would vomit if she opened her mouth, so she clenched her teeth and shook her head.

The nausea died down.

"Shouldn't we hold funeral rites for her," she murmured almost to herself. "Throwing her away in the cargo hold is too much."

The man agreed. There was nothing in the patrol ship that would do for funeral rites, however. Even if there were, neither of them would be able to find it in the short time they had left.

They took her body to the airlock instead, laying her down by the outer hatch and the two of them standing by the inner one. She pressed a button and the outer hatch opened. Isfobeddin's body slid out of the hatch and floated out into blackness.

For some reason, she thought of the river of the white planet.

"I'm sorry," she whispered toward Isfobeddin's body.

They closed the outer hatch and returned to the cabin.

"Do you know how to land this thing?" Indigo Skirt asked when she came back.

Of course she didn't. Light Green Skirt looked at the man. He also looked perturbed and shook his head.

"How are we going to land?" said Indigo Skirt to no one in particular.

She looked at the man.

"Why are you looking at me?" he said. "The course is already plotted and I assume the ship will know what to do to land."

"The Imperial language, you can read?" she said.

"Do you think reading is the only thing you need to know to land a spaceship?"

Red Sword

"Better than not knowing anything," said Light Green Skirt, taking her side.

The man looked up at the ceiling and sighed. He began to walk.

"Where, going?" she said to him.

"The control room."

The patrol ship shook. Both Light Green Skirt and Indigo Skirt fell over Dark Green Robe.

She managed to right herself just in time as a loud noise spread through the ship. It was a human voice, but not a language she could understand. She and the women, surprised, kept looking at each other until the man came running back inside the main cabin.

"Come over here, quickly," he said, and for a moment she only stared at him, lost as she was in the sudden shaking and the noise.

"What?"

"I said, come!"

She ran after him.

Her face filled the screen in the control room. It was expressionless and kept saying something in a disinterested, measured manner. But she didn't know what she was saying.

"What's meaning?" she asked the man, but he looked as confused as she was.

"I don't know. Tell her to speak in your language."

She turned to the monitor and shouted, "Who are you!"

The herself in the screen said something. Her voice was so loud it made the room vibrate, but she couldn't understand her.

She shouted again, "What are you saying? Talk in a language I can understand!"

She looked off to the side of the face that looked like her. She took a step back from the screen.

Behind the woman who looked like her was a whole line of women who looked like her. They were all wearing uniforms she had never seen before. Not the gray of the Empire nor the white of the aliens.

The patrol ship began to turn.

"Endless …" She stared into the screen that was filled with her. "But why. …"

"They must have a remote control system," said the man who had misunderstood her question. "We're being brought back."

She had reflexively turned her head to him when he spoke but didn't really hear his words. She looked again at all of her faces that filled the screen. The twisted smile on the face of the woman who looked like her with whom she had fought sword to sword. *Surrender now, and I'll let you die more comfortably*. The taunting, the hate in her eyes. The shock when she was pierced in the stomach, giving way to oblivion when she was shot in the temple with the gun.

The woman in the screen was not the one she had killed. It was another, new her. This face and all the faces behind her were cool, emotionless, almost peaceful.

She looked down at herself, at what she was wearing. The gray uniform of the Empire. The tears in places matched where Light Green Skirt had been injured, with her trousers stiff in places with the blood of the young man that had congealed in lumps.

It wasn't over. The people who mattered to her, the people who had tried to kill her, so many had all been hurt or killed, but it wasn't over.

Red Sword

She slid her hand into her pocket and brought out the blue-green key. Carefully, so the screen wouldn't see it, she handed it to the man. He glanced at what she was handing him and looked up at her.

"I can't go back," she said. She looked him in the eye and spoke in the language of her long extinct people. "There's no way I can go back. And I don't want to go back."

The man's face went from confusion to understanding. Then, grim determination.

He stealthily accepted the key and pressed it under his palm as he scanned the panel before him. There was a slot with the same symbols engraved on it as the back of the key. Casually, keeping the key in his palm, he moved it to the slot, leaning against the panel and turning his head away from the screen.

Before he dropped the key into the slot, he looked at her. She nodded.

The face on the screen had no time to register what was happening before he quickly moved the key in his hand and slid it into the slot.

The patrol ship keeled. They fell on top of each other and slid across the floor, hitting the wall. Before she could get up, the control room flipped over completely. Something hit her face, then her shoulder, hard. She fell down to the control room ceiling. She tried to find the man, reached out her hands for him, but instead of his hand, a hard and sharp thing grazed her forearm, cutting her. Right before she lost consciousness, she thought of her sword and the embroidered, red scabbard. For no good reason at all, she thought of the blood that had soaked her blade when she pierced the woman who looked like her. The image came to her, clear and sharp.

She crashed.

Someone was shaking her awake and speaking to her. Her body wasn't moving. Were her eyes open or closed? Her eyelids weren't moving and there was only darkness before her.

"Atung," shouted the shaking person. "Where is Atung!"

She managed to open one eye. The other eye was covered in something wet and heavy.

Indigo Skirt. Not the one who had just crashed with her on the patrol ship, but the woman who had disappeared during the spaceship battle on the white planet. Trying to focus her eyes, she looked up at the woman bent over her. She could just about make out a large wound covering a side of her face.

In the main cabin, your lover is in the main cabin, she wanted to say. *She's searching for you, she was searching for you this whole time, she risked her life to find you.*

She couldn't find her voice. She tried to get up—her body wouldn't move. When she tried to turn her head, her neck and shoulders and temples felt like steel bars were running through them. When she managed to move her head a little bit, she could see a steel fragment coming out of her abdomen.

"Don't move," whispered Indigo Skirt. "Where is Atung?"

Because she couldn't answer, she moved her eyes. But she didn't know where the main cabin was at this point, because she didn't know where she herself was.

Her voice still refused to come. Her mouth gaped and she struggled with her breathing. She wanted to talk about many things. About the battle, about the white aliens' base, which surely wasn't too far from where they were. About everything Dark Green Robe had to go through to find Indigo Skirt. About her swordfight with the woman who looked like her, cutting off the life support of the young man who had still been alive although cut in half, about tricking Isfobeddin to her death by using the names of her children. She wanted to talk about it, to cry about it, to scream about it. For none of these were fake memories transplanted into her, they were her memories and hers alone, her very own life. And now, as the blood and her life flowed out of her, those memories, and those moments would all vanish.

She thought of the man. She realized she still didn't know his name. It was too late now. She would never know it.

She stared up at the sky. The whiteness was covered in black blotches. She was witnessing her final moments as the light in her eyes went out. But because Indigo Skirt looked up and seemed to see them as well, she realized what those blotches were.

Imperials. The Imperial reinforcements had finally arrived, having crossed immense space and taken many years. She remembered the people who looked just like her, the ones who wore the unfamiliar uniforms and spoke in an incomprehensible language.

"Sword …" she whispered. "My sword …"

She tried to get up. She coughed. Blood spurted from her mouth.

Indigo Skirt stood up, staring at the sky.

"Run …" she said to her. "Sword …"

She managed to sit up. The steel fragment remained in her

stomach. She coughed, one hand on the fragment so it wouldn't move from her coughing, and the other hand searching the ground. "My sword …"

She stood up. Struggling, swaying, and just barely with the help of Indigo Skirt, she hugged her torn body to herself, and stood.

There was no sword. She was empty-handed. Still holding the fragment in place, she looked up to the sky with great effort.

Indigo Skirt took her free hand and squeezed it tight. She squeezed back.

It was just the two of them left. There was no sword.

She turned to Indigo Skirt.

This is the end. There is no retreat.

Indigo Skirt looked back at her, and as if she read her mind, nodded slightly.

The two women turned forward, still holding hands, and gazed as the Imperial ships blasted the earth with white light, splitting the sky.

Red Sword

©sangsangsquare

Bora Chung has written four novels and a whole lot of short stories. She has an MA in Russian and East European area studies from Yale University and a PhD in Slavic literature from Indiana University. She translates modern literary works from Russian and Polish into Korean. Among her works, *Cursed Bunny,* a collection of short stories, was shortlisted for the International Booker Prize in 2022 and was a finalist for the National Book Award in the translated literature category in 2023. She currently resides in Pohang, South Korea.

Credits: Anton Hur

Anton Hur translated *Cursed Bunny* and *Your Utopia* by Bora Chung, *The Underground Village* by Kang Kyeong-ae, and co-translated *The Age of Doubt* by Pak Kyongni. He is the author of *Toward Eternity.*